## PRAISE FOR JUSTICE IN A BOTTLE

"'It's never too late for the truth,' insists Nita, the plucky heroine at the center of Pete Fanning's novel *Justice in a Bottle*. An aspiring investigative journalist at the age of thirteen, Nita doggedly pursues the answers to her burning questions, despite resistance from her school principal, her classmates, her mother, and her talkative internal critic. This is an inspiring story about a young girl's passion and perseverance, beautifully told."

Clifford Garstang, Library of Virginia Literary Award Winner

# JUSTICE IN A BOTTLE

## PETE FANNING

*Appropriate for Teens, Intriguing to Adults*

Immortal Works LLC
1505 Glenrose Drive
Salt Lake City, Utah 84104
Tel: (385) 202-0116



Cover Art by Ashley Literski
http://strangedevotion.wixsite.com/strangedesigns



ISBN 978-1-7339085-8-0
Ebook ISBN 978-1-7923-2355-3

*For Simon.*
*Go find your story.*

Nita Simmons sat in Mr. Abrams' office, trying to slink low in a chair designed to prevent slinking. The morning sunlight taunted her from the window, flickering through the budding dogwood branches and splashing onto her principal's hunched shoulders as Nita's favorite teacher defended her credibility.

"As I've said, Nita's story has been retracted, removed from the website. She's written a full statement along with an apology," Mrs. Womack said, handing over the statement.

Nita's gaze fell to her lap. The words "retraction" and "apology" pricked like needles on her neck. When she managed to look up, she found Mr. Abrams' bulging eyes peering over his eyeglasses, regarding her the way one might regard a splotch of mustard on a shirt.

The principal clutched the statement a few inches from his nose. Mrs. Womack, also the editor of the school newspaper, had gone back and slashed and cut what Nita thought to be the clever parts. Nita shifted in her chair. Sure, she'd screwed up big time, but Mr. Abrams didn't have to seem so eager about it.

While this was her third year at Crawford Middle School, it was her first visit to the principal's office. She could have sworn there was an air of victory in his voice as he lowered the page.

"We expect more from you, Nita." Mr. Abrams tossed the statement and jabbed a pudgy finger at a printed copy of the original story—a four-hundred-word exposé about a giant sinkhole in the school's parking lot.

Nita cleared her throat, forcing her eyes to meet the principal's. "I know."

"Just what were you thinking? Barging downtown, challenging your own school administrators no less, with these... these phony accusations? I mean, the stunt you pulled with Coach Meyers was one thing, but this..."

He trailed off, as though he was too disgusted to finish the thought. Nita shook her head. She had no excuse. She'd been so sure of the Stallworth piece, so itching for a controversy that she had misread reports, ignored logic, and plunged ahead, alluding to a cover up. When the blowback came—and boy did it ever—Nita pushed back, claiming her first amendment rights were under attack. She'd marched downtown and demanded the admins release what they knew. And so they did, which happened to be groundwork plans for new water supply lines.

"Well, this should do," Mr. Abrams muttered, shifting back to the statement.

Nita opened her mouth, ready to squeeze in a few words in her own defense, but Mrs. Womack caught her eye with the slightest shake of her head.

Nita unclenched her jaw. Her gaze fell to the floor. "Thank you, sir."

"Very well," Mr. Abrams said, adjourning things.

Nita got to her feet, nodded. Mrs. Womack turned for the door, Nita close behind, when the principal cleared his throat.

"Nita, if I may. Why don't you try covering a sporting

event? Maybe the school dance? You could try your hand at a fun spring fever story? Something positive for once?"

Nita blinked. The needles returned to her neck, hot and sharp. Next up for her was an op-ed piece on mass incarceration. But there would be no next up, not after this. Nita sucked a breath, about to dig her own sinkhole and bury herself when Mrs. Womack set a hand on her shoulder. "Oh, we have a few stories lined up. A couple of leads."

Mr. Abrams' phone began chirping. "Very well. But remember Nita," he said, shaking the paper at her. "Be more careful with your words from now on."

In the halls, word of her flop spread. While *The Chronicle* mostly went ignored on a weekly basis, since Nita had flubbed the Stallworth piece news was flying off the desks. Nita kept her head down. She pretended not to hear the snickering in the halls. A few of the boys on the bus had the nerve to ask her what she would report on next. *Mudslides? Radiation? A new ice age?*

Whatever. Nita could deal with the jerks. What worried her more was her membership to the Junior Journalists Club. In her rush to glory she'd violated every core tenet of the club. Last week, she'd been sure she was on her way to the big time. Now she might have to cover a volleyball game.

Off the bus, Nita slogged down the sidewalk with her head down, the weight of her worry heavy on her shoulders. High on the hill, Nita usually enjoyed the splendid view of the river snaking through downtown. She knew her town's history. At one time, her house, like the others on the block, had belonged to the wealthy folks. Long before the floors were divided, the doorways walled off, the fireplaces sealed, and the crooked mailboxes labeled 2*A* and 2*B* were slapped onto the sagging porch. Before the wealthy took their views someplace else.

But today Nita wasn't thinking of urban decay or abandoned vistas. She muttered to herself about retractions and statements, climbing the last splintered step to the porch when a booming, thunderclap of a voice greeted her.

"Who in the world are you talking to, child?"

Nita stopped cold. Because for one, Mr. Earl Melvin of 2B was outside in plain view, yawning like a bear fresh out of hibernation. Two, Mr. Earl Melvin of 2B had dragged out a rocking chair and what looked like a wooden fruit crate to the porch. And three, not only was Mr. Earl Melvin of 2B outside— a first—he'd chosen today of all days to speak to her.

Normally, Nita wasn't short for words, but normal had never gotten out of bed that morning. Not after the day she'd had—was still having—with her neighbor out there talking to her. Normal had skipped town altogether. Nita had nothing.

She snuck another quick glance at him. Though they'd never spoken to each other, Nita had grown accustomed to the old man in a certain way. She always knew when he'd come or gone by the prickly aftershave scent lingering in the foyer. She could set her alarm his TV would start blaring at six and go silent at eight. And his rumbling coughs were about as common as the radiator pipes banging around between the walls on a cold night.

Being a journalist, or ex-journalist as it was, Nita knew all too well what people said about Mr. Melvin. Something awful that happened right in Crawford years ago. How he'd spent twenty years behind bars at Jamesway Correctional. *Just their luck*, Nita's mother had said when they'd moved into 2A last fall. She'd been asking the landlord to change the locks ever since.

Now, Nita thought she saw the makings of a smile on the old man's face—a face that reminded her of a car missing its hubcaps. Like he was waiting for her to come sit and talk to him. Nita snorted. He was too old to be waiting so long. And who was he calling *child?* she thought, even if she had been talking to herself. But all of that was forgotten once she saw the old notebooks piled up on the wooden crate by his side.

Mr. Melvin smacked his lips. "You keep it up and people might start thinking you're crazy, Miss Nita."

He chuckled. Nita did not. But the way he said her name, *Miss Nita*, set her back. She eyed him more carefully now, her legs poised to kick or run, depending. Finally, with a curt nod, Nita moved for the door. "Yeah, you're one to talk," she said, cinching up her backpack and scooting past him.

Once inside, Nita couldn't help another peek at her notorious neighbor, rocking along, humming a tune. The notebooks at his side. Strange.

She took extra care to flip the deadbolt to her apartment. She flopped down and attempted to do her homework at the table. Didn't happen. Between the meeting with Mr. Abrams and the Earl Melvin sighting—he'd actually spoken to her!— Nita's brain was in no shape to conquer math.

When her mother came home almost an hour later, Nita didn't mention the whole retraction thing at school. She fought off the urge to ask her mom if Earl Melvin was still out on the porch. Those kinds of questions would only get her mother going about changing the locks again. And her mother would only agree with Mr. Abrams about covering "something positive" for the paper.

So Nita said her day was fine. Just fine.

They were in the kitchen when Nita's mother rang the wooden spoon three times against the pot on the stove. She gave Nita a look. *That* look.

"Homework done?"

Nita's mother asked her about homework every day, even on Sundays. And every day and even on Sundays, Nita told her she'd done most of it.

"Math?"

Nita sighed.

Her mother raised her eyebrows, repeating the question in the form of a threat. "*Math?*"

Math books made Nita's head hurt. All those numbers and fractions and word problems. It was enough to make her dizzy. Besides, she knew the basics, she always knew when Mr. K down at the market had short-changed her. But square roots and cube challenges? After the day she'd had? She got through three and gave up.

Thinking of school meant thinking about the newspaper. And thinking of the newspaper sent her mind reeling back to the Stallworth mess. And thinking about the Stallworth mess led her to the Junior Journalists Club.

"Hey, Mom?"

"Yes, Nita?"

"I need to pay my dues."

"What dues?"

"For the JJC."

"Well, do you have any money?"

"Um, like two bucks."

"How much are the dues?"

"Twenty-five."

Nita's mother feigned astonishment in such a way Nita wondered if she had ever auditioned for theater in high school. Nita was sure she'd mentioned the dues for the club months ago.

Her mother shook her head. "That's a lot of money, Nita. Aren't there any free clubs you can join?"

Nita halted her eye roll. She knew what was coming, a sermon about how the water bill was late or the phone bill was due or how they would have to get the car inspected. Sure enough, her mother sighed. "I swear, one thing after another around here." She turned back to a cloud of steam on the stove.

Last month it was the muffler and before the muffler it was the battery, now she went on about the tread on the tires. Nita's mother worked at the insurance company up the road, answering phones. To Nita, it sounded like torture, listening to a bunch of cranky people screaming in your ear about insurance rates all day, but her mother had told her once how she'd learned to tune them out after a while. Sometimes Nita suspected her mother was tuning her out, too.

After dinner, Nita bundled up her dirty clothes and headed for the laundromat. With all the newfound attention at school she wanted to be sure her clothes were cleaned and pressed. She figured she could at least look credible, even if her writing was not.

On the porch, Nita found the old man's rocking chair empty and still. She shook her head and got on her way, choking on the thick April pollen that was like chalk on her tongue. The evening sun bounced off the upper rows of windows, lending hope to those raggedy buildings and life to the dandelions springing up in the patches of dirt.

As she plodded along, the teasing faces at her school were still etched in her head. She thought again about the Stallworth piece, the retraction. At first, she'd offered to quit the paper. But Mrs. Womack would have none of it. Instead, Nita vowed never to let it happen again. But she couldn't get over the fear that it would.

Speaking of fears, there was the Junior Journalist Club. Nita was thirteen, and a whole summer away from high school, but she already had her plans mapped out. Her plans did not include the JJC rescinding her membership. Not only over the dues, but the pledge. The pledge Nita knew by heart. The pledge to seek the truth. To fight injustice. To always use better judgment to better journalism. That last one was trouble.

Nita dropped her head. She'd been looking forward to the

end of the year convention ever since it was announced last fall. On the website, she'd clicked through picture after picture of last year's event with all the smiling faces as members dressed up fancy, trading war stories, winning awards, and otherwise basking in the spotlight. They'd even met with real reporters. How could she have been so careless?

Her thoughts spun with her clothes. With her two dollars spent, Nita packed up. She took her time getting home, crossing the bridge as the sky squeezed the day pink in the distance. She climbed the hill with weary resolve, to the splintered porch, to the old house where the light glowed inside a tangle of cobwebs, dimmed by the impressive collection of bug guts in its bowl. She reached for the wobbly door handle when Mr. Melvin's notebooks caught her eye.

Nita figured the old man must have forgotten them. She let her laundry bag slide off her shoulder, missing its warmth as her clothes fell to the floor. She zipped up her sweatshirt and edged closer to the crate, thinking back to the odd encounter with her neighbor. What he'd said, the sound of his voice, what everyone said he'd done.

A few runners slogged by, traffic drifted along while some early bird crickets chirred. Another peek at the door and Nita reached for the rocker. The arms of the chair were shiny and smooth, worn through the paint.

She eyed the broom and dustpan in the corner, where the old man had staked a claim to one side of the porch. Another look over her shoulder and she picked up a notebook from the top of the stack, because she just had to see what it was all about. Then she stopped.

*To use better judgment...*

Nita knew a thing or two about respecting privacy—even a convict's notebook filled with all sorts of dirty secrets. She bit her lip. She'd hate for something to happen to them, even if they were already soggy and smelled of must and mildew. It was the least she could do to bring them in, maybe drop them at his door.

She leaned over to gather the others when the cover of the one in her hand fell open. The pages were filled with scrawl, the letters so rippled and gritty on her fingers she thought they might slide right off the page and through the planks.

Her eyes widened at the first words she saw.

*The noose was tight, scratching and clawing at my neck. Demon eyes pinning me down like I was nothing more than a rabid dog…*

Nita's head popped up. Her brow curled and her mouth hung open. Another glance over her shoulder, to the foyer, then back to the notebook. Privacy took a back seat. Nita flipped through to another page.

*Guilty. Guilty before trial. Before Mary ever spoke to me. Guilty at birth.*

Nita's arms puckered with chill bumps, bumps that had nothing to do with the falling sun, and everything to do with what she held in her hands. Then came the itch, the itch Nita got when she needed more. When she had a story.

It was getting too dark to read. Nita leaned closer, trying to catch the porch light on the page, trying to make out the dangerous, slanted words in neat cursive when the porch light went out.

Nita froze. Footsteps in the foyer. Her mother, the old man, either way it was trouble.

*Guilty.*

Nita slapped the notebook shut and stuck it behind her

back. She ducked to the side just as the door creaked open and Mr. Melvin shuffled out, grunting and humming. Nita's body tightened in the dark as he hobbled to his freshly swept corner.

While seeing him earlier had given her a jolt, now, in the gray of dusk, as he settled in his chair with rumbling hums dragging with the beat of traffic, Nita thought he looked like any old man on any old porch. Still, she cursed herself for being so nosy.

The humming grew louder yet softer, in time with the rocking chair. Nita felt his voice on the bottoms of her feet, climbing up her legs and tickling her back. He struck a match and the flames danced with each puff—a sweet cherrywood scent filled the night.

Shaking out the match, he settled in with a grunt and said, "Good evening, Miss Nita."

Busted. Nita swallowed hard and forced herself from behind the swing. She looked to the door once again for her mother, hesitated, then crept out towards the old convict. She held the notebook out to him—the notebook filled with strange, dangerous words.

She took a deep breath to steady her voice. "So what's this all about?"

# CHAPTER 2

"Ah, I see you've taken to my memoirs," Mr. Melvin said.

Nita nodded, her eyes darting from the man to the door. A puff on the pipe. A few ragged coughs, a gravelly chuckle, then another puff. Again a quick cough, the squeak of the chair. Cough. Puff. Squeak. Faraway voices behind the chirp of the crickets.

Eyeing him up close, Nita studied the deep wrinkles of his face, the sprigs of white hair. He reminded her of a painting better viewed from a distance. She realized she was still clutching the notebook.

"Is this... is it really true?"

With the pipe in his teeth, he turned his palms up. "It's all true, Nita. I'm an innocent man."

*Innocent man?* No sir, not from what she'd heard. Or what she'd read. But the words on the page, they stole her breath, how he'd scrawled the word *Guilty* over and over and over until it sounded like gibberish in her head.

Traffic was scarce. The streetlights lined the empty sidewalk, cutting a path between the tiny lawns and the street.

Mr. Melvin started again with the humming, a deep but soft melody like he had all night. Nita did not have all night. She thought about how much trouble she'd be in if her mother busted outside and found her talking to the man she'd warned Nita so many times about.

And yet, Nita couldn't help herself. She waved off the thick smoke blanketing the chilly spring night. She shifted, her hand found her hip. "If you were innocent, why did you go to...?"

"Prison?"

He said it without remorse. Like it was the Hilton.

Another glance at the door. It never occurred to Nita that she might be more afraid of her mother than the town's most notorious convict. Across the bridge, the purplish clouds had surrendered to the night sky. Mr. Melvin chuckled until he coughed, then he coughed until Nita thought he might fall out of his chair. By the time she'd had enough and decided to leave him right there to choke, he stopped, slapping the worn rails of his rocker. "Oh Nita, that's a good story. A real good story."

NITA LAY in bed the next morning, reliving the encounter as she stared at the cracked plaster above her head. She heard her mother shuffling around in the kitchen. Nita figured she must have slept okay because her footsteps were light and easy and without the thunder they carried when she was fussing. Nita closed her eyes, enjoying the easy hums in the other room, until she remembered how her mother had jumped down her throat for getting back so late.

But the morning sun, its promising light in her room, made last night seem like a dream. Nita heard the front door squeak open then pull shut. A moment later her mother's car grumbled to a start and Nita rolled out of bed to get ready for school.

Even as she told herself it didn't bother her—the kids laughing in the hallways at school—it was starting to wear her down. She heard the whispers, the hushed laughter. She saw Queen Alexis and her friends over her shoulder in the mirror, judging her wardrobe, snickering and giggling, igniting a rash of stinging down Nita's neck.

She found a striped button-down shirt to go with the jeans she'd washed last night. She tilted her head in the mirror, scrunched up her nose. Lately she'd been eyeing her mother's mascara but hadn't worked up the nerve to use it. No time for her hair, she stuck a clip in it and got on her way.

Somehow, Nita knew Mr. Melvin would be out there, even though before yesterday she'd never seen him on the porch. His whistling fell flat as she stepped out, and he did something with his mouth that could've been mistaken for a smile.

"Looks like another day is upon us."

"Hope it's better than yesterday," Nita muttered. He'd straightened up the stack of notebooks, or memoirs, as he'd called them. The very one she'd held in her hands on top. Should she apologize for going through his things? Or had he left them for her? Nita's journalistic mind wandered with questions. What else had he written in there?

The skin on her arms prickled once again. She kept her eyes on the worn path in the carpet on the porch, the frayed edges of loose threads twisted and curled like little worms on the street after a hard rain. Down the block, Earnest waited for her. She gave Mr. Melvin a small wave. "Well, see you later," she said, trying and failing to drown out the rampant curiosity flooding her brain.

She hit the steps when Mr. Melvin cleared his throat. "And Nita?"

Nita wheeled around as though he'd reached out and grabbed her shoulder. The morning sun glinted in his eyes and filled the deep grooves in his skin. Nita thought about him last night. Dark as a shadow with that flame in his hands. *I'm an innocent man, you know.* Only this time he did smile. "Don't let them get to you, okay?"

Nita couldn't help but smile back. She wasn't sure who or what he meant, but she liked the way he said it. She tossed him another awkward wave and set off down the street.

Earnest Calloway had his head down as he scanned the sidewalk for treasures. From what Nita could see, it had been a productive morning for her dumpster-diving friend. On the curb, next to his book bag, were two water-logged science-fiction books and a paint brush, slightly used.

Nita picked up one of the books. "Ah, *Space Lobsters II.* Classic."

Earnest straightened and glanced over her shoulder towards the porch. Earnest never looked anyone head on, his gaze was either on the ground or dreaming in the sky. But what Nita liked most about Earnest was how he said what he was thinking. In fact, he was the most honest person she knew.

Earnest nodded to the porch. "What were you talking to Earl Melvin about?"

Nita flipped through the book. She shook her head. "I'm not quite sure."

Earnest squatted, peeling a filthy lottery ticket off the street. Nita rolled her eyes. For four years she'd known Earnest, and in those four years she'd seen him gather more trash than the city dump. Every bottle cap considered, any scratch ticket double checked. Coffee cups, receipts, magazines—even fast food bags had to be searched for coupons.

Earnest set his eye back to the curb. "I'd be careful, Nita. You know what they say about him. And your mom would kill you if she—"

"Yeah, I know," Nita said. Again, everyone in Crawford

knew about Earl Melvin and his terrible crime. But what was she supposed to do, now that he'd taken to the porch, walk right past him every day without a greeting? Rude. And those words he'd written were now pinned to the "Must Know More" corkboard in Nita's brain.

She peeked back at the porch where Mr. Melvin was rocking away. "You know, I think," she started, knowing she could never say what she was about to say to anyone else, "I think he might be trying to say he didn't do it."

"Really?" Earnest looked over at the porch, then he shielded the sun with his hand as he turned back. "Well, that would be quite the story, wouldn't it?"

She swallowed the urge to scratch her itching curiosity. She reminded herself what Mr. Abrams had said. Finally, she gave her friend a shrug. "I hadn't thought about it much."

On the bus Nita took her usual seat and leaned against the window. She did some of her best thinking there, gazing out at the new day as the engine groaned and growled under her feet. Today, Nita had lots to think on, thanks in part to Mr. Hack, the Editor-in-Chief who resided in her head. Mr. Hack had been around since the sixth grade, popping up at the worst times. He spoke in a rapid, old timey accent, and Nita knew from experience he wouldn't stop until she followed his advice.

*Nita, I think we've got something here.*

"No, we don't," Nita whispered, slipping down in her seat. She'd been determined to ignore Mr. Hack ever since the Stillwater debacle. Easier said than done, however, because Nita knew she did indeed have something. And soon enough she was off, brainstorming about Mr. Melvin and fifty years ago. How last night his voice was thick and smooth but this morning it had sounded rough, like an engine that hadn't quite warmed up yet.

*We do, Nita. We've got something big. You know it. I know it. And I know that you—*

"Fine. I'll read the memoirs. But it ends there." Mr. Abrams had been clear.

While Mr. Hack muttered his grievances, across the aisle, Earnest sat slouched, sorting through the soggy paperback. Nita smiled. Her mother thought Earnest was strange, how he didn't say much and avoided people's eyes and all, but it never bothered Nita. She took it as a challenge, like she had to earn his attention. He'd all but shut down when his brother died, and Nita figured he'd talk about Terrence when he was ready. And yeah, Nita thought, he might be strange, but who was she to judge?

She spoke to a voice in her head.

After class, Mrs. Womack reminded Nita about the op-ed piece. The one on mass incarceration Nita had been researching before yesterday's meeting with Mr. Abrams.

"I thought I was covering the volleyball thing," Nita said, in no hurry to face the nonsense in the hallways. She laid her arm across the desk, setting her head in the crook of her elbow with a yawn.

Mrs. Womack laughed her off. "Very funny, Nita. Honestly, I think you'd make a terrible sports reporter."

Nita smiled. Her head popped up. *Mass Incarceration. Falsely accused.* Her mind flashed to Mr. Melvin, and all his talk about being an innocent man.

Mrs. Womack raised an eyebrow. "Are you okay, Nita?"

"What? Oh, yep, I'm fine."

"Don't look so worried. I won't make you cover the game."

Nita forced a nod, emerging from her thoughts. While she loved how Mrs. Womack leaned on her for real topics (the rest of the staff wrote those movie reviews or video game critiques Mr. Abrams craved), with real topics came real deadlines.

And consequences. For the first time in her life, Nita found she was afraid to write. Every word was screened and nixed inside her head before it ever had a chance to come to life. She felt like the whole school was watching, waiting for her to flop again. And it wasn't helping how Mr. Hack kept blathering on about Mr. Melvin and those memoirs. It was going to be near impossible to buckle down and get back to work.

"Nita?" Mrs. Womack's voice went serious now. "Why don't you stay back after school? I can help you out if you'd like."

Nita shook her head. "No, it's fine. I'm uh, I actually do have something to research." A real journalist did not get help from the teacher. A real journalist made deadlines.

At lunch, Nita braved the cafeteria. She ate with Tamika and Tamika's new friends, who spent most of the period going on about some Insta-drama. Pushing through her taco salad, Nita, too distracted to contribute to this crisis, caught only bits and pieces of what was being said. "...so, yeah, she's not speaking to Amelia because of that..."

Boring as the conversation was, Nita was thankful for the distraction. She doubted Tamika and her friends even knew about the Stallworth piece, being that they were too busy mapping out their destinies as the next global pop stars.

While Tamika had her life all figured out, Nita was no longer sure about her own path. She thought back to the day she fell in love with journalism. She was at home, sitting on the floor watching the news when the camera panned across a war-torn country in the Middle East. She'd sat up close, pulled to the screen where she found the impeccable Ingrid Houston, braving the winds, standing strong and resilient in the chaos and destruction. Her scarf swirled about her face and her jacket plumed behind her head, but her eyes remained fixed, piercing through the sand and fog, pinned on Nita as she spoke.

And that was it. The determined eyes, the poise, the compassionate voice had fascinated Nita. Ingrid Houston was risking her life for the story, yet she was unwavering in the howls of war. For Nita, the gears had clicked into place.

Here was someone who looked like she did, someone who maybe even could have been from Crawford, Virginia, out there, pulling the story from the rubble of decimated homes still smoldering after being bombed only moments before. Ingrid Houston gave those victims a voice, spreading not only news, but hope with her words. She traveled all over the world, chasing danger and refusing to back down. She was strong. Nita would be strong. This was what Nita wanted. No. This was what Nita *had* to do.

And she had never looked back.

Until now.

That afternoon, Nita almost walked right past her own porch—something she'd done before while sorting through a story. But today she almost passed her own porch because the old spindles and railings were scraped clean of the cracked and peeling paint. Out front, the flower beds were clear of all the leaves and trash, making way for the green tulip stalks peeking out from the dirt. A pile of old chairs sat at the curb, along with bags of leaves, and the rolls of faded sun shades and dusty rugs that had been on the porch since Nita had lived there. Someone had even managed to haul the old boxy air conditioner out of the way.

Nita took the stairs, admiring the tidiness of the now spacious porch. She almost didn't see the old man, folded over in his rocker, chin to chest with his eyes slammed shut. *Is he even moving at all?* She eyed the paint scraper laying on the rug at his side, like it had fallen from his fingers. A trail of paint crumbs down his shirt to his boots.

A careful step. A look back. Then, clearing her throat, Nita approached her neighbor the way one might approach a hornets' nest. "Mr. Melvin, are you... are uh..."

Her foot hit a squeaky plank. One eye flew open.

"Oh," Nita said, a hand to her chest, catching her breath, "I was just making sure."

"Making sure I wasn't dead?" Mr. Melvin blinked to life, rubbing the arms of his chair. He smacked his lips and looked around, as though he wasn't all too certain himself. "Nope, not yet. But that air conditioner nearly killed me."

Nita chuckled. She waved a hand over the spindles. A birdfeeder hung behind the porch swing. "Did *you* do all of this?"

He nodded, then coughed, then wheezed, then clutched his chest like he was going to rip his shirt right off his body. When he got through with all of that, he rubbed the rails of the chair, his eyes catching the sun with a squint. "What, you didn't think an old man could do some heavy lifting?"

Nita couldn't help grinning at the old man's grumpiness. In a way he reminded her of Grandpa Simmons. The few times she and her mother had made the drive to visit her grandparents, Nita always made it her mission to get a smile out of her crusty grandpa. And most of the time she managed, even as her mother and grandfather only managed to argue over money.

Nita shook her head. "No, I just... well it looks nice, is all."

He nodded. "Yes sir, figured this place needed some sprucin' up. All those years of inspections and what not, you learn to keep clean quarters."

Inspections. As in jail. Nita took a small step back. She glanced around, noticing how the crate was missing. The notebooks were gone. Mr. Melvin hummed along. "Yep, still got some more to do. Figure I'll paint tomorrow. That nurse who always comes around pestering me said I need to get out more, get some fresh air. So if I'm going to be out on this porch, might as well have things cleaned up some."

Nita set her hand to the door handle. The old man grumbled and his head dipped again to his chest. She waited for him to say something about guilt, or innocence, but he only closed his eyes. Nita stepped inside.

She ignored the deadbolt. She tossed her book bag to the floor and turned on the television. She turned the volume up high to drown out what she knew was coming.

*What kind of journalist gives up like that?*

Nita shook her head and sighed. "It's called patience. Building trust. I didn't give up. I'd call it a breakthrough."

*I thought it was a missed opportunity.* Uh... it looks nice... uh... uh... uh... do you, *Ugh, I've heard pigs oink more articulately.*

Nita tore into the bag of chips on the table. "Please shut up. I mean, don't you have some black and white PSA to narrate?"

*As a matter a fact I do, it's called, Grammar 101. Heard of it?*

"You are so annoying. But since you're here and won't leave me alone, did you happen to hear anything about the Stallworth piece? The one you were so worked up about?"

*I did, it's a shame, kid. Oh well, win some, lose some is what I say... although I still think they're covering their behinds.*

"Ugh." Nita slammed into the seat at the table. On TV, an infomercial blared about perfect skin and easy payments. Nita thought about mass incarceration. She thought about Mr. Melvin and being innocent. She ate semi-stale potato chips. She drummed her fingers on the table and attempted to do homework. She thought about her essay and threw herself on the couch and told herself she wasn't a real journalist. She reminded herself once again how horribly she'd screwed up, that no one would ever take her seriously.

After a while, Nita heard the front door open with a squeak, followed by the heavy sweeps of the old man's boots in the foyer. Nita stood and started for her door, where she could almost feel the old man as he shuffled past. She heard the jingle of his keys. So many questions. Mostly about the notebooks. But then his door creaked open, and Nita took a breath, thinking about what had happened the last time she thought she was onto something, the mess she'd caused.

Nita held still. And Mr. Melvin's door clicked shut.

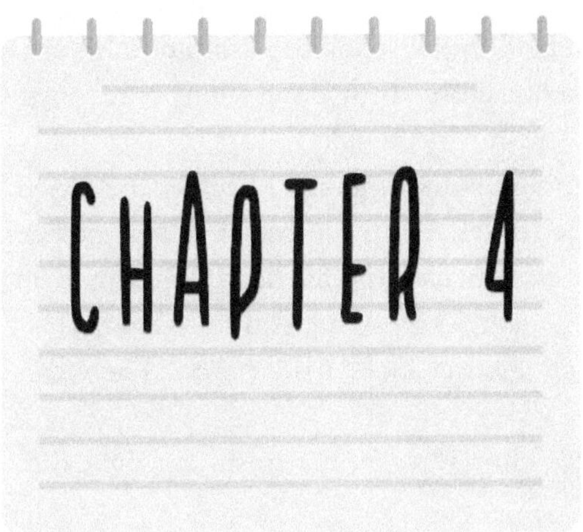

# CHAPTER 4

The next morning, Nita stepped out on her porch and found Earnest pacing up and down the sidewalk in front of her house. He popped up when he saw her, his eyes widening with a smile so big Nita thought she could dive into it.

He was up to something. She hadn't seen Earnest grinning so big in a long, long time. And she, too, grinned as she skipped down the steps and blocked his path. Earnest stopped short, almost crashing into her. She crossed her arms against the chill, still trying to bury her smirk. "Okay, so what's with you?"

He looked up, chewing on that smile of his. His head made the trip to Nita's neck but his eyes peeked up to meet hers before dropping to his feet. "I found something."

She looked at the trash from the porch, then to her friend's worn sneakers and argyle socks, his green and yellow rugby shirt and how the sleeve cuffs stopped short at his wrists. She'd been taller than Earnest until last summer. Now he had a few inches on her, easy.

Earnest tried to sidestep Nita but she cut him off again. She cocked her head. "Spill it, E."

He fiddled with the strap of his bag, once again smiling like crazy. Then he flung his book bag around to his chest, unzipped it, and came out with Mr. Melvin's four notebooks. "Okay, and uh, you're welcome by the way."

Nita's smile fell. She glanced back at the porch, working to keep her voice down. "Earnest, you stole his notebooks?"

He was already shaking his head. "I did not *steal* anything. He threw them out. And again, you're welcome."

Nita took another look at the porch. The clean porch. "He did not."

"He did. They were in the trash can right there, sitting on top."

"What?"

Earnest pointed to the beat-up garbage can. Nita thought about spring cleaning, the crate, sprucing up or whatever the old man had been yammering about. Earnest handed over the notebooks. How could he throw them out?

They started for the bus stop, just a block down the street. Nita held the notebooks close to her chest. "We can't keep these, Earnest."

Earnest held up his index finger. "Allow me to bring you up to speed, Nita. It's called public domain. Are you familiar with California V. Greenwood?"

Nita rolled her eyes. Unperturbed, Earnest continued, "The Supreme Court ruled it to be, and I quote, 'common knowledge' that garbage left out on the street is readily accessible to members of the public."

While it made her smile listening to Earnest and his inexhaustible knowledge of trash, Nita clutched the notebooks as a war of ethics raged in her head. She ran her thumb over the spiral bind, where some of the pages had torn away. She felt the history at her fingertips while her friend rattled on about the fourth amendment and legal warrants until the bus appeared in the distance.

They hurried to the bus stop, where Nita could see that Earnest had been busy. Mr. Melvin's crate lay by the curb, spilling over with treasures. Electrical wires, a busted-up collection of gold door knobs, hinges, springs, and a metal drill with a frayed cord. Some golf balls.

The bus lumbered to a stop. The door opened. Earnest picked up the crate. "Well, aren't you going to tear into them?"

Nita looked back at the porch. She set the notebooks in her book bag, zipped it tight, and tossed it over a shoulder. This felt like something to read in private, not on a bus full of dumb kids shouting and teasing her about sinkholes.

"Yes, but..." Nita smiled as Earnest nodded for her to go first, his crate of trinkets jingling as he struggled. She closed her eyes and shook her head, but then turned back. "Thank you, E."

"Hey, no problem."

School became background noise. All Nita could think about were the notebooks. She set them in her locker, but not before she stole a quick peek at a random page.

*It was no big surprise when the county boys in overalls and boots came calling. I expected the pitchforks and torches, the hound dogs and pick-up trucks. They would always come for the likes of me. What caught me by surprise was the housewives and churchgoers, the respectable folks clutching babies and little kids. How they pointed and glared at me with vengeance. Folks who quoted scripture. Even the preachers, teachers, well-to-do folk. They saw me and their eyes hardened, spit formed on their tongues.*

Nita jumped at the sound of the bell. She scrambled off to class, leaving the notebooks behind in her locker for safe keeping. But the words remained in her head, ticking like a bomb, and by lunch she was swimming upstream through the halls, hurrying back to pick up the first notebook from the stack and stuff it into her bag.

Nita rushed off to the library, a place where she was famous for waiting lists and late fees. She found her favorite desk vacant and calling to her from the far corner near the reference materials. She collected her breaths. The notebooks looked a little more worn and yellowed and out of place in the school. On the desk. She opened the cover and breathed in the musty traces of tobacco and coffee and twenty years of hard time.

*I first met Mary at Crawford Memorial Hospital. She worked in records and filing. I was a porter, on the nightshift, content to clean bathrooms with hopes of getting promoted. This was in the fall of 1964... and I had no idea that promotion would never see the light of day. But oh, back then, I thought I was on my way...*

The rest of the day was lost on Nita Simmons. Because she couldn't stop there, she spent the next few days (and nights) sifting through Mr. Melvin's most private thoughts. At night, she flopped around in her bed as she grappled with the pledge. *To seek the truth.* Check. *To fight injustice.* Check. *To always use better judgment to better journalism.* Um... to be determined.

As Nita read through the first notebook she took notes. Mary Werrins and Earl Melvin had a special connection from the start. She covered her laugh when she read how Mary loved Earl's corny jokes. How Mary's dimples bloomed when she smiled. Dimples that only made Earl Melvin learn more corny jokes.

Nita read when she was supposed to be reading *A Tree*

*Grows in Brooklyn.* She read in the kitchen, after walking past Mr. Melvin on the porch. Reading the notebooks instead of doing math homework was a no-brainer, because anything was better than math homework.

Her op-ed went untouched. Even as Nita reminded herself the Melvin thing, whatever it was, wasn't a story. But if it was, if Mary and Earl were, well, together, *that* would be the story of a lifetime. Something sure to bury that sinkhole business once and for all.

Nope. Again, not a story, but since Nita was the only person in Crawford on speaking terms with Mr. Melvin, she knew it fell on her to get some answers. And on Friday morning, with her mother at work, she stepped out onto the porch, trying her best to appear cool and calm. Until she blurted out, "Good morning, Mr. Melvin."

Nita cringed, because her voice came out too high and bright, like the whine of an eight-year-old.

"Miss Nita," he said, through a pipe full of smoke—which Nita thought defeated the whole fresh air thing, but she needed to stay on topic.

"Good morning," Nita repeated with a wince. Then, in an attempt to be casual, "Oh, hey, where are your notebooks?"

Mr. Melvin peered over the morning newspaper. He didn't look to be in the mood for chatting. He didn't look like a man who'd ever told a joke in his life. He made a show of folding the paper and shifting to face her. Nita knew she'd blown it.

The old man looked down. He looked right, then left, before waving it off. "Reckon I need a fresh start. No point in dwelling on the past."

Nita couldn't believe what she was hearing. She glanced down at the bus stop, where Earnest motioned for her to hurry. But Nita wanted to make sense of what the old man was saying. "Okay, it's just that, well, you said they were your memoirs, right? I mean, we can learn from the past, can't we?" Nita was impressed with herself for such quick thinking. "And all that stuff you were saying the other night, about..."

His eyes drilled into her. "You mean my innocence?"

A wicked grin carved lines in his face. Nita's foot tapped. She managed a nod before she looked back to the street. Two blocks away, she could see the flashing red lights of her school bus.

"Yes." Nita said, torn now. She felt like a flag dangling from a tug of war rope, swaying from the steps to the old man, back and forth. The bus closed its doors. Earnest waved frantically for her to hurry.

The old man shifted. And while Nita might be the only one speaking to Mr. Melvin, she knew she had no control over what was being said. He started to set the pipe in his mouth, then stopped short. "Let me ask you this, Nita. Why do you care what was in those notebooks?"

Nita lifted her head and forced herself to meet her neighbor's foggy eyes. She'd heard him say *was*, even as the notebooks were in her book bag—sitting heavy as an anvil on her back.

She gave up trying to match him riddle for riddle. She sucked down a breath and shook her head. "Because I believe you, all right? At least, I mean, I *want* to believe you, even if it sounds crazy, being as I hardly know you. But this has been a pretty crazy week, and well, I don't know why, to be honest... but," Nita paused, because the words were tumbling. And she couldn't say she had the notebooks, could she? "I guess I can't stand knowing something like this happened."

Mr. Melvin leaned back with a squint, his mouth on its way to a smile but not there yet. The bus rumbled down the street. Earnest looked like he was doing jumping jacks, his arms flailing over his head. The old man stared at her for a moment, long enough for Nita to feel foolish about what she'd said, then he grunted, snorted, and nodded to himself.

"Very well," the old man said with a chuckle that reminded Nita of the gears on the bus. He waved a hand towards the curb. "Tell you what, you go catch your bus and get to school. I'll be here, Lord willing, when you get home. We'll talk then."

Nita nodded. But her feet didn't get the message. *That's it?* They seemed to say. Nita wanted to sit there and talk to him all day. But the bus was coming, pulling up to her stop, so she sighed. "Okay. But I'll be late today, because it's Friday and I need to stay back and..."

The old man nodded out to the street, chuckling along. "Looks like you better get going."

"Oh, right," Nita said, flushed from all her babbling. Some journalist, she thought to herself, hustling down the steps and rushing off to catch the bus.

# CHAPTER 5

Nita found Mrs. Womack in her class after school. Mrs. Womack's eyes shined. They always shined. Even after school on a Friday—especially after school on a Friday. Mrs. Womack greeted Nita with a bright smile.

Nita's eyes dropped to the floor. She never missed a deadline. And now here she was, showing up with nothing but faith. After a retraction, no less.

Where was Mr. Hack when she needed him most? When she'd been sitting in the principal's office, he'd been out to lunch. After talking Nita into chasing down another wild story, he was nowhere to be found. Nita stood completely alone, with nothing to show for herself but the buzz of emptiness in her brain. Well, maybe not emptiness, the conversation with her neighbor was still echoing around up there.

Mrs. Womack held out her arms. "Well?"

Nita sighed. "I need an extension."

Mrs. Womack waved her off. "Nita, you can keep the laptop as long as you need."

Mrs. Womack kept a laptop in her room, a loaner for

students on assignment. The "loaner" could be checked out for one week at a time, for classmates in a pinch. But Nita couldn't help noticing how hers was the only name down the rows on the log. Everyone else had a computer, and Nita figured out long ago that Mrs. Womack did this for her. At first, she'd been embarrassed about it, but then she only became all the more determined to be the best.

Nita closed her eyes, her toes curling up in her shoe. "Thanks, but I meant for my piece."

Mrs. Womack lowered her head to get Nita's full attention. "Nita Simmons wants an extension." She clapped her hands and popped back up. "Oh, this must be good. Oh, this is better than good."

Nita looked up. Mrs. Womack's bright red smile poked and prodded at the corners, daring Nita to smile. She did, but it didn't last. "It's... I mean, after what happened last time, well, I'm not so sure..."

Mrs. Womack wouldn't hear it. "Listen, I know you may have some doubts right now, but I want to tell you something." She took a seat at the edge of her desk. "You are an excellent writer." She glanced around the room, then lowered her head and whispered, "Probably the finest writer I've ever taught, okay? There, I've said it."

Nita tamed the second smile, but her heart leaped. She stared at her feet so she didn't look like a dog begging for a treat. "Tell that to Mr. Abrams," she sighed.

"You have a gift, Nita. You also have a ferocity that's sometimes needed to get a story. Oh, and stubbornness, you've got that, too, by the truckload." She stepped forward and found Nita's eyes. "Extension granted."

"Thanks." Nita's smile grew. "Okay, so I might have something, but..."

Mrs. Womack stood up straight and smacked her sides. "I knew it!"

She had Nita now. The way her eyes shined with inspiration, they challenged Nita to wow the world. But how? She had no story, not yet anyway. Nita picked up a pen from her desk, clicked the clicker a few times and smiled, her voice returning to normal. "Well, it's going to take time. It might be an explosive piece."

"Oh," Mrs. Womack said. "You mean I just made that confession, talked you off a ledge and here you were sitting on some big story the whole time?" She smiled. "Okay. Extension still granted. I suppose we can get by with the fluff in the meantime."

Nita followed Mrs. Womack around her desk, where her teacher wiggled the mouse and the screen came to life. "I've got a few movie reviews, and there's the new Justin Bieber album..."

Bieber. Movies. *Ha, I've got the story of a lifetime,* Nita thought in her best Mr. Hack impression. Wait, where did that come from? Nita reigned herself in. She thought of sitting in that chair as the principal admonished her recklessness. How earlier that morning she'd stood on the porch spilling her guts to her neighbor instead of asking questions.

Nita bit her smile and nodded. "It's local," she said, baiting her teacher. "It's uh, it has to do with an important piece of Crawford's mired legacy."

Mrs. Womack raised an eyebrow. *Mired legacy.* Ugh. That's what Nita got for impersonating Hack. But Mrs. Womack smiled. "Sounds good." She held up two fingers. "You've got two weeks, Nita, bring me something good."

*Oh I have good, all right,* Nita thought.

She had something groundbreaking, maybe. But did she have the tools to dig it out? To get the old man to talk? And even if she did, did she have the chops to unearth the story and set it free? The courage to take on another big story and risk the wrath of the school again? Because what if she was wrong again? Or worse still, what if she was right and no one cared?

She hopped off the activity bus and shuffled down the block to find that the old man had been at it again. The porch spindles glistened wet and white, shining in the fading sun. She approached the porch, her feet more certain than her brain.

This time, Mr. Melvin was wide awake, although he didn't seem so happy to see her. Nita fingered the zipper to her book bag. She didn't know what to do next, how to begin or what to say, but she felt like she'd passed some sort of test when he nodded and said, "Good afternoon, Nita."

Nita had thought a lot about what he'd asked her, about caring so much. And to be honest, Nita was still trying to figure that part out herself. But she knew in her gut Mr. Melvin's story needed some attention. Sure, she'd keep her distance for now, even though Earl Melvin no longer seemed scary or dangerous, but a little rough around the edges. The way Nita saw it, if Ingrid Houston could brave bombs and war and windstorms, Nita could get some answers out of Earl Melvin—even though it seemed he was getting more answers out of her.

He leaned his head back and fought to take a deep breath. His crackling wheeze sounded like someone balling up a newspaper. "You know, what you said this morning, about believing me? Well, it got me thinking and I decided maybe you were right, that some stuff is worth keeping." He gazed out at traffic. A few sparrows found the bird feeder, pecked, looked up, pecked again and flew off. "In fact, I figured I'd go retrieve my notebooks."

Nita's face flashed hot. She closed her eyes and when she opened them he was waiting with a nod. Shoulders slumped, Nita unzipped her bag and pulled out the first notebook. The glint in Mr. Melvin's eyes sparked. His brow narrowed and the specks of paint in his hair took a ride with his scalp.

She gave him her best smile. "Mr. Melvin, are you, by chance, familiar with California V. Greenwood?"

The old man chuckled into a cough. He went through the usual bedlam of hewing and barking, and when he was finished he smiled and leaned his head in. "Can't say I am. So was it you or that boyfriend of yours digging through my garbage?"

Nita's ears caught fire. She shifted, broiling in lava-like mortification, somewhat irritated with the old man's teasing. "He's not my boyfriend. And full disclosure, I'm reading these."

Mr. Melvin nodded again, his gaze never leaving the notebook in her hands. Nita wiped back her hair and shifted to face him. Time to get cracking. She pounced.

"You say they came for you." Nita straightened her back, shifting gears and finding her voice. "Was it because they thought you'd done, um, *something* to Miss Werrins?"

"*Something*, huh?" He swung his sagging brown eyes up to meet Nita's. "All I did was love Mary."

Nita stumbled on his words. A chill hit her arms and she knew it would be easier to stop. To get inside and leave fifty years ago alone. She could work on her mass incarceration piece. Or a movie review. Even volleyball. And that's when Hack showed up. *If we're going to do this, Nita, ask the questions. Ask him—*

Nita swallowed. "Was it because Miss Werrins was white?"

The way he flinched said it was. A cough scraped his throat and again Nita thought maybe he should ease up with the pipe. He wiped his mouth with a rag from his pocket. "What do you think, Nita?"

Nita held firm. "I told you I believed you."

"Okay." He grunted, nodded, then began. "This was right

over across town," he said, breathing heavy, his chest rumbling. "I thought for sure I was dead. *Knew* I was dead."

Nita forced a nod. He glanced out at the traffic. She was still staring at his profile when he turned to her. "And you know what? I wasn't even scared."

Nita raised an eyebrow. "You weren't scared?"

Mr. Melvin shook his head. "Nope. Well, I wasn't scared of *them*. By then I wasn't scared of much of anything. I'd already thrown it all away, *because* of fear."

He was talking in circles. Not only that, Mr. Hack was back, yapping away.

"Okay, but um..." Nita took a breath. Between the riddles and Hack and all the thoughts flying through her head she couldn't get the words out. She wiped her palms on her lap, set her hand on the notebook. Mr. Melvin pulled out a pocket watch and checked the time. It was scuffed and cloudy in places but still holding onto a shine. He was still coughing and didn't look so hot. His eyebrows hung low and grouchy, and Nita knew her time was up. Sure enough, after some grumbling, he wiped his mouth and turned to her.

"Nita, I think I know what you're after, and while it's awfully nice talking to someone after all these years, I think that's about all it's worth. Talk." He motioned to the notebook. "You're welcome to read what's in there, but then I think we should let it go, got it?"

*Let it go? Nita, if he's innocent, I mean really and truly innocent, well, we could be talking Pulitzer here!!!*

"Shut it."

Mr. Melvin, turned a sharp eye to her. "What's that?"

"Oh, not you. I mean. Sorry." Nita shook her head to reset. What a mess. And not only that, she thought about what might happen if her mother caught her sitting out there with *The* Earl Melvin. Another wipe of the palms and she slid from her seat and tried to exit with a morsel of professional courtesy. "Okay, Mr. Melvin, but if what you're saying, I mean, you're the one who brought up being innocent and all." She tapped the notebooks. "I mean, well, I guess what I'm trying to say is that it's never too late for the truth."

A click in his throat, Mr. Melvin shook his head. "Oh Nita, me and the truth parted ways years ago."

On Friday morning, Alexis Evans—bully, mean girl, Facebook poster of a link to Nita's retracted story with the caption, "Fake News"—spent the first few minutes before class bemoaning how "some people at this school had no sense of style."

It didn't take an investigative reporter to figure out the *some people* Alexis Evans kept referring to was Nita. Not with those little sideways glances. Not after she "whispered" to Carolyn about how she'd stepped in a sinkhole the other day.

Nita couldn't imagine what Queen Alexis might say if she knew Nita's lip gloss came from a dumpster—even if it had still been in the plastic. Earnest had given it to her last week at the bus stop, along with some still packaged hair clips and a head band. Nita thought it was nice of Earnest, even if she knew *some* people would disagree.

Nita rolled her eyes and found her book. Alexis was the least of her problems, although thinking about style and lip gloss did get Nita thinking about the JJC convention. There was the issue of finding the right dress (or finding the money to buy said dress) for mingling about in some fancy ballroom at the nation's capital. Several awards, including a scholarship grant—The Pentip Award for Excellence—were to be presented and, according to the rumor, some of the industry's leading journalists would be in attendance.

Leading journalists, as in Ingrid Houston. Nita's head dropped. She was without an essay, couldn't pay her dues, had a fresh retraction under her belt, and was now chasing some chicken scratch folktale story based on four notebooks worth of scrawl. There wasn't enough dumpster lip gloss in the world to fake her way through this one.

Nita went back and forth on what to do. The old man's story was glued in her head all week, everything she'd read so far, about Earl Melvin's jokes and Mary's dimples, about how the hunched man on her porch had once been so full of hope and love (and jokes, wow). Only now the whole town thought he was crazy. But he was talking to her, and that had to mean something, right?

He wasn't scared of *them*, he'd said. But then he said it was because of fear that he'd thrown it away—whatever that meant. His story was confusing, no doubt, but the problems Mr. Melvin had faced made Nita's flub seem less world-shattering in comparison. Still, he'd said he wouldn't do the story, so where did that leave Nita?

His reluctance wouldn't have stopped the old Nita. The one who'd talked her way right into the mayor's own living room seeking answers about a city council decision to forgo salary increases for city workers, including teachers. But that girl had been a different Nita. One with confidence and swagger. One who had never asked for an extension. One who'd never been to the principal's office.

So she hid in the library. She read, she sulked. She stared

out the window. She managed a C- on her math quiz. It was a day worth forgetting.

What Nita needed was some cheering up, so it was only fitting she found Earnest in his usual spot on the bus, curled in his seat and making some headway through *Space Lobsters II*. Nita stopped at his seat. Beside him lay a plastic tray of soggy cupcakes. Without peeling his eyes from the book, he scooted the tray Nita's way.

"Cupcake?"

A cupcake—even ones with all the frosting folded to the side—was exactly what she needed. Nita took the tray and plopped down beside Earnest. Carefully, they peeled away the plastic wrap as the bus grumbled out of the parking lot and up the hill.

Nita looked at her friend with a smirk. "Do I even want to know?"

"The lunch lady and I have an understanding." Earnest set the book aside.

"I'll bet you do."

Nita found two cupcakes with most of the frosting still in place. Without hesitation she took a bite, and she had to admit, it was hard to stay down in the dumps with a mouthful of cupcake.

They rode side by side the whole way home, stuffing their faces, smiling like goofs without saying a word, knees knocking together occasionally. And it was with frosting on her cheek that Nita decided she needed to change her approach if she was going to get the old man to play along. She had to convince him to let her do the story. Because this was a story now, Nita knew as much.

Nita's mother came through the door in a gust of sighs and agitation. She complained about work, about rude people, about the potato chip crumbs Nita had left on the floor and the books and notes and index cards scattered across the kitchen table.

Nita was only saved from her mother's wrath about messes and chores when her mother's phone buzzed in her purse.

Nita watched her mother's face change as she took the call. How it brightened and she laughed. How she became a new person in an instant. When she launched into what may have been the most boring conversation in human history—top five at least—about who had said what to whom else at work, Nita couldn't help but roll her eyes.

Sometimes Nita wished she was more like her friend Tamika. She wished she could talk pop music or dance because then maybe her mom would take more interest in what was going on in her life. But whenever Nita tried to watch a mind-numbing fashion show or music videos, her mind wandered off to research or stories. Sometimes she'd float off into her own world, she and Hack, writing up silly pieces in her head.

Nita could only guess this was her father's doing, the way she could get so completely wrapped up in her own thoughts. Only, when it came to Nita's father, all she had was a guess. Talk of her dad was off limits in the Simmons' household—Nita's mother refused to discuss it. Besides, any mention of it put such pain in her mom's eyes Nita couldn't bear to bring it up. Of course, Nita was doing her own research—she knew her mother had been in love with one boy throughout high school—and one day she'd find the courage to seek him out.

*Research.*

*Story.*

*Deadline.*

Nita scooped up her notes and headed to her room where she kicked off her sandals and plunged into notebook number two.

Mr. Melvin and Mary Werrins were taking risks. Driving the dirt roads in Mary's car, windows down, the wind loud, tossing Mary's hair all over the place, flying into Mr. Melvin's face as they cut through the countryside. Nita had to remind herself it was her neighbor who had written what she was reading. Mr. Melvin wrote how he told jokes because he loved the sound of Mary's laugh. How hard it was to keep finding ways to be alone. At work or during the day before their shifts. On their days off. All the time.

Last year, Nita had watched two documentaries on the Civil Rights movement. She knew some about the gruesome lynchings that had plagued the Jim Crow south. She'd read about the bombings in Birmingham and all the awful things that could happen to people because of the color of their skin. She'd read about the lunch counter sit-ins and the success of the bus boycotts.

Then in her own town, at Crawford Park, Nita had walked along the grassy field, edged in concrete, where a pool had once stood. A WHITES ONLY pool drained and filled with concrete years ago by city officials after local civil rights leaders scheduled a "wade in."

But even knowing all of these things, Nita wasn't prepared for what she read.

*There were some close calls. Like the time I got Mary's Buick stuck in a ditch. I pushed and pulled but it was no use. We sat stranded and panicking for a few hours before a pickup truck came bouncing along the road. A couple of hunters, of all things, dogs yapping in the back, rifles on the gun rack. They slid to a dusty stop and I knew it was over. Knew it.*

*They regarded me like something to shoot at, but Mary was quick on her toes. She told those hunters I worked for her, that we'd been out running errands and gotten lost. Mary fluttered her eyelids and just like that they rushed to help, pushing and shoving her Buick out of the mud. Next thing we knew, they'd tipped their hats and gotten on their way. We laughed about it for the rest of the night.*

Hard to believe they would continue to take such chances. That Mr. Melvin would sneak flowers into Mary's locker, only to hear Mary's coworkers laughing and gushing over which doctor must've been so crazy about her. It was their secret. Sharing lunch in the janitor's closet, quick, hidden smiles in passing, writing notes in a code only they understood. Each stolen moment was magical.

They couldn't help themselves.

Mary Werrins and Mr. Melvin were in love. And they took chances. They weren't safe. And something else Mr. Melvin had written stuck with Nita. He'd said love was stupid to reason. Love wanted to be heard, to be seen, it wanted to be shouted from the mountaintops.

Nita rubbed her eyes. She tried jotting down some notes but her mind was dizzy and her breathing came jagged and fast. Her neck tingled and her shoulders were sore from sitting so tight. Fist clenching, she felt the hope sitting between each word, the fear living and breathing between each page. And although Nita was just beginning to understand her neighbor, she was now starting to put it all together.

Mary was in love with Earl Melvin, and she'd wanted to shout it from the mountaintops. Mr. Melvin was in love too, but he'd been told all his life to whisper.

# CHAPTER 1

On Saturday morning, Nita set off for the public library. The cherry blossoms stamped the sidewalk, and she hugged her sides against the cool, damp breeze. She passed the park, thinking how it felt more winter than spring, and even though the early morning was gray and dreary, Nita knew Earnest would be out looking for treasures.

Earnest had taken it hard when his brother passed. The whole town took it hard. It was just before school began last summer, and Terrence was a star football player at Sampson High. Mr. Calloway, Earnest's dad, loved more than anything to brag about how good Terrence was and where it might take him.

Every Friday night, the Calloway family used to get all decked out in their matching team colors as they set out for the stadium to cheer Terrence on. Earnest used to keep all of Terrence's stats in an old composition book. He'd tell anyone who asked how many tackles Terrence had, how many interceptions he had in a season, everything. Then one day Terrence collapsed in practice—something with his heart—and just like that there were no more stats to collect. Ever since then, Earnest kept his head in those dumpsters.

Nita found him near the basketball courts, roaming around the picnic area where he liked to look for scratch tickets.

"What's up Earnest?"

He turned his head with a nod. He wore Terrence's old football jersey to go with red plaid shorts and a black winter hat with ear flaps. Nita fought off a smile.

"Aren't your legs cold?"

Earnest shook his head but something caught his eye. He bent down and pulled out a wrinkled lotto ticket. "Look, a free play."

"Cool." Nita stuffed her hands in her pockets. The clouds, low and gray, smothered the sun. "Hey, I'm headed to the library, you want to come?"

Earnest shrugged. "Sure."

They started up Fifth Street and Nita settled in for a quiet walk with her friend. But he turned to her. "You aren't going to quit are you?"

Nita felt the morning chill in his words. "Quit what?" she asked with a chuckle. Because they both knew. She let out a big breath of steam, let her arms fall and her shoulders sag. "The Mr. Melvin thing? I don't know. He doesn't want to talk, and even if he did, after the Stallworth thing, I mean, what is Mr. Abrams going to say if I follow that up with this? I can see it now." She framed the imaginary headline with her hands. "THIS JUST IN, EARL MELVIN FALSLY ACCUSED OF…"

She let her hands drop. She still couldn't say it.

Earnest shrugged. "If anyone can write his story, it's you."

Nita's stomach squeezed tight. Her smile broke through. "Thanks, E, but I'm supposed to be doing movie reviews or music or… volleyball."

Earnest skipped along, his gaze pinned to the ground, scanning, searching. "I think you should stop being so hard on yourself. I mean, yeah, the sinkhole thing turned out to be a bust, I guess. But what about the teachers' pay raises thing you did back in the fall?"

Nita's face warmed. She closed her eyes, shook her head with a smile. "You remember that?"

"Yep. And all the teachers do too, I'll bet."

The strength returned to Nita's strides. Just hearing Earnest talking so much was enough. The nice words about her was an added bonus. "Thanks, E."

He shrugged. They crossed the street and she got Earnest talking about his latest adventures. He'd already hit the dumpsters behind the Dollar Plaza and scored a broken radio. Nita just wanted to keep him talking.

"Do you ever get in trouble or chased off, I mean, from stores and stuff?" Nita asked, nodding to the radio.

A small spark hit Earnest's eyes. "Yep. Sometimes. But it's worth it." He held up the radio with a frayed power cord. Nita laughed. Another trophy for his collection. She'd been to Earnest's house, during better times. Earnest had his own workshop in the basement garage, filled floor to ceiling with junk.

They arrived at the library, a stately building sitting defiantly amongst the payday stores and rent-to-own centers, the bus station across the street. It was often crowded out front, people milling around, waiting to use the computers or read the newspaper. And while Nita could take care of herself, Saturdays were always busy, so it was kind of nice having Earnest around. Even as he was drifting off, a magnet pulled away by the force of recycling bins and all that public domain. Nita shook her head and laughed as Earnest looked back and waved.

Nita smiled. "Have fun."

By Monday, Nita was back at her regular lunch table and feeling the pressure. She'd done zero research and never even got a chance to convince Mr. Melvin to let her do the story. She stirred her pasta with a plastic fork. Mr. Hack had been quiet all day.

She did her best to listen as Tamika went on about her dance troupe, but she was thinking how she'd almost knocked on Mr. Melvin's door on Sunday. She'd even made it out to the foyer with her notepad and recorder. She'd turned left but stopped before knocking. Running into a strange old man on the porch was one thing, banging on his door and bugging him could prove dangerous. The man had been in prison, after all.

Nita sat at the table, tapping her feet and spacing out as Tamika talked dance. Then Earnest passed, balling his face up and crossing his eyes at Nita.

Nita snorted, spitting her drink all over the table because she wasn't expecting that from Earnest. Tamika turned around and when her eyes went big, Nita knew she was in trouble.

"Hey, what was that?"

"What?"

"You know *what*." Tamika gave Nita a glossy smirk. She'd been wearing makeup since last year, and it sort of bugged Nita how she always acted like she was older and wiser when it came to such things. Tamika nodded towards Earnest. "Your boyfriend back there."

Not this again. Nita shot her a look. "He's not my boyfriend, T."

"No?" Tamika grinned. Nita's face went hot. It felt like her hair was on fire. Why was Tamika always making a such big deal out of things? Tamika glanced over her shoulder again and smirked.

Nita's ears were about to melt. "No. I mean, I don't *like* him," she said, managing to peek up from her tray. Her cheeks must have joined her ears because Tamika clicked her tongue and grinned.

"You like the weird ones, huh? Speaking of, you've been acting weird yourself lately. I saw you walking the track yesterday, out there mumbling to yourself. What's up with that?"

"I wasn't..." Nita stopped, unable to convince even herself.

Tamika glanced back at Earnest. "Sort of cute, I guess."

"Don't," Nita almost begged. Something about Tamika calling Earnest weird didn't sit right with her, even if he was by a mile. But cute? Well, Nita asked Tamika something about dance just to change the subject. And the mumbling? She'd take it up with Mr. Hack later.

Nita split the rest of the day going back and forth between what to do about Mr. Melvin and what Tamika said in the cafeteria. Things only got worse on the bus ride home, when Earnest slid his dirty book bag off the seat to make room for her. Nita paused, but then walked right past him and plopped down near the back.

She stared out the window the whole way home. When the bus slowed at her stop, she stood and started for the door. Sometimes Earnest got off and walked down with her but Nita couldn't force herself to look his way to see.

She felt a hitch in her step but powered through, even as somewhere in the ten conversations buzzing around she could feel her friend's quiet stare on her back. Her face flushed. Hot ears again. Why did Tamika have to make such a big deal about everything?

*ita. Wake up, Nita. This is no time for sleep. There's work to do.*

Nita blinked to life. She recognized the source of this sunrise harassment. Mr. Hack had always been an early riser, and now he was banging around her head like he'd had too much coffee. She rolled over and pretended she hadn't secretly missed his urgent voice.

*So here we have an innocent man, heartbroken, judged by his peers, and thrown in jail. And you're going to waste your time sleeping?*

Nita pushed up on her elbows. "Okay, first of all, we don't know for sure. Secondly, it was fifty years ago. And lastly, I'm not wasting my time with this." She flopped down, yanking the blankets over her head in an attempt to drown out the voice... inside her own head.

"Ugh." Nita flung the covers off and again pushed up on her elbows. "Where have you been, anyway?"

*Have you done anything without me? Have you interviewed*

*him? Have you even written a word? Honestly, Nita, I'm disappointed in you.*

Nita ignored Hack the best she could. She got dressed and crept out to the kitchen where her mother buzzed about, humming and singing. Nita poured a bowl of Raisin Bran and took a seat, surprised when her mother plopped down at the table.

She wiped at Nita's hair, picked lint from her shirt. Touched her just to touch her. "So, what's new with you? I've been so busy with everything I feel like I haven't seen you in a while."

Nita broke from her thoughts. She took a breath, about to let it out when she realized she'd never even told her mother about the retraction—ancient history, it seemed. Little good it would do now, with Mr. Hack sounding alarms in her head about the Mr. Melvin thing—which, she could downplay it all she liked but it was *a thing* now.

She took a bite of the dark flakes, dripping milk on the table because it's impossible to eat Raisin Bran without spilling milk. "Well, I'm trying to come up with an essay for the Pentip Award. Um, that and I'm working on another piece for the paper. Sort of."

Nita's mother shot her a look. "Since when have you ever *sort of* worked on anything?"

Where Nita couldn't sit through one of her mother's TV shows, her mother would never understand her daughter's passion of journalism. Nita cocked her head with a smile, spooned another bite of cereal to buy some time before plodding ahead.

"Well, it's going to take more research. But it's something close to home."

Just like that, her mother yawned. She went for her phone and began scrolling. "Oh, sounds interesting."

Nita set the spoon in the bowl. She knew she'd lost her

again. Nevertheless, she was trying to think of a way to bring up Mr. Melvin—if nothing else it would give her conscience an alibi—when her mother's brow furrowed. She shook her head and sighed. "Oh lord, looks like Sunnyside was robbed again."

Robbed again. The muscles in Nita's neck tightened. Her toes curled. She thought about the past repeating itself. About last summer and Mr. K's boarded up windows and all the police cars and craziness. She nearly leaped from her seat as her mother's phone rang. A quick look at the clock on the microwave.

Time to go.

NORMALLY, Nita would have been buzzing about a possible story, but her mind clung to the contents of the memoir in her bag. And she couldn't resist spending her lunch reading in the library then returning again after school to make notes.

In fact, Nita managed to make a pile of notes. She even put the Sunnyside Market out of her mind, at least until she arrived home to an empty porch and an empty apartment. Inside, she found a note, scribbled on an old receipt. Something about mandatory overtime. While overtime might be great for all those overdue bills on the counter, it was bad for Nita's nerves to be home alone with nothing more than her galloping imagination about robbers on the loose.

The police had no suspects and no leads, and Nita had no idea when her mom might be back. After a half-hearted attempt at homework, Nita took to the third notebook. Only she had trouble concentrating. The worry stayed in her chest, pulling and squeezing. She got up and peeked out the door every few minutes.

She paced. She flipped through the channels. She did her

best to ignore Mr. Hack—still going on and on and on, suggesting Nita get off her rump and do the interview.

"Right. The interview. Let me remind you, *Hack*," Nita said, spinning on her heels and waving her hands as she spoke to herself. "An interview requires one person to ask questions, and the other—willingly, I might add—to answer those questions."

*Very good. Say, you might make a decent reporter one day.*

"Ugh. You know what?" Nita snatched her recorder from the table and stomped to the door. She took a breath and stepped out into the hall where every snap and squeak in the floor had her jerking her head around like a bad actress in a scary movie.

*Almost there.*

"This is crazy," she said, eyeing the door that was worn through many layers of paint. The peep hole. The speckled door handle. She held up her hand to knock but stopped.

*He's dying to talk, Nita. Trust me on this.*

Before she could chicken out, she set her knuckles to the wood, twice, holding her breath as the door rattled in place. Slow, heavy steps shuffled across the floor on the other side.

*That a girl, Nita.*

"Shh."

"Who is it?" Mr. Melvin said with such force Nita felt it in her feet.

She swallowed down the fear and found her voice. "Um, it's me, Mr. Melvin. Nita Simmons."

Her voice sounded small and squeaky after his bellowing, and she jumped again at the scrape of the chain on the other side. *Last chance to run,* she told herself right before the door swung open and Mr. Earl Melvin stood before her like a wilted stalk.

*Straighten up. Stand tall and look him in the eye.*

His faded button-down shirt was missing a button. His

khakis worn to a shine. He rubbed his face and blinked like he'd been napping. This time when he spoke, his voice was softer. "Everything okay?"

Nita looked back to the entranceway of the house, an old glass door that couldn't stop a gentle breeze from getting inside. Then she forced herself to meet the old man's gaze. His eyes, under an awning of bushy gray eyebrows, were a little cloudy but focusing.

"Did you hear about the market?"

He nodded, looking over her shoulder and down the hall. "News said something about a robbery. You weren't down there were you?"

"No. But I was hoping..."

*Don't back out now, kid. You're right there, on the cusp of breaking this thing wide open...*

"Be quiet," Nita muttered under her breath.

"Excuse me?" Mr. Melvin said, his face scrunching into a mess of wrinkles.

"No, I mean, not you..."

Mr. Melvin peered over Nita, looking down the hallway. "I thought I heard you talking to someone next door."

Nita squeezed her eyes shut. She bit her lip and shrugged. "I was wondering if we could talk?"

Mr. Melvin's face softened. He looked down at her recorder and smiled. "Talk, huh?" he grumbled. Nita waited for him to send her packing. Instead he opened the door wider. "Okay, we can talk. Come on in."

From the first glimpse inside, Nita was amazed. Then, the smell. Like sticking her nose into her grandmother's china hutch, only with a faint aroma of a pot roast lingering in the kitchen. The walls were covered with frames of black and white pictures. Baseball players, boxers, men in bowties, a woman playing piano onstage. Another wall held built-in shelves, rows of books and records.

*Okay, we're in. Just act casual...*

"Easy for you to say," Nita whispered.

"You want something to drink?" Mr. Melvin called, heading around to the kitchen, stealing her attention away from the wall. "All I got is water," he mumbled.

"No thanks. I'm okay."

Nita stood in front of the open door, only now noticing the local newscast in the boxy television, sitting on the floor like a trunk. Another glance around, the room was cozy and inviting, washed in a golden light from a corner lamp. But Nita wasn't sure whether to take a step in or back. She could *feel* the eyes on her from all over the room.

Mr. Melvin returned with a beer in his hand. Oh boy. Nita pushed away the red-hot image of her mother's face. Mr. Melvin started to close the door but Nita took a step back, instinctively, clutching the recorder. "Um..."

The old man stopped short. He nodded his head. "You know what? Probably best we leave this open."

She watched as he took a giant book, grunted as he leaned forward, and dropped it to the floor with a thud. "There."

Nita smiled, half ashamed and half relieved. But she was consumed once again with those faces on the wall. The rows of books. The shine on the floor and the warmth of the room.

Mr. Melvin hobbled over to his chair. "Okay Nita. You've got your recorder ready. Let's talk."

*Told ya, kid. It's Pulitzer time.*

Nita took a breath and stepped inside. Mr. Melvin took to his armchair and gestured to the small couch. She sat, set the microphone near Mr. Melvin, and pressed record. "Okay, I have more questions regarding Mary—"

*Stay with it, Nita.*

"Just hush," Nita mumbled.

Mr. Melvin leaned over and shot a fierce look at Nita, then back over his shoulder to the open door. "Who are you talking to?"

"No, I'm, nothing. No one."

The robbery. The overtime. This fascinating room. Nita was off her game. But if Mr. Melvin, the strangest of them all, thought *she* was strange, well, then what did that say about her? "Um, I'm sorry, I was... see it's..." She cleared her throat. "So, um, have you spoken to Mary Werrins since?"

*More specific, Nita...*

"Since your release."

Another sip of beer. A smack of the lips. "Can't say I have."

"And you were released in..." The notebooks hadn't mentioned his release. The notebooks hadn't mentioned much of anything after Mary.

The old man shot her a look. "1985."

Nita was dying to know what he'd been doing all this time, but she didn't want to push. Besides, his evasiveness only brought on more questions. Was this his idea of talking? She sighed. "Oh. Okay. Um, how come you never appealed your conviction?"

"I think a group of lawyers did." Another sip. Smack. Shrug. "Denied."

He crossed a leg, then uncrossed it. Drained his beer. Nita turned away and spotted an old battered guitar in the corner. It was without strings but worn smooth from use. A television commercial filled the silence between them. Nita chewed on her bottom lip. This was Hack's fault, rushing over like this, unprepared. Her questions out of order. She was flustered, a failure. She wasn't a real journalist and he knew it. Everyone knew it.

She took a deep breath and closed her eyes. Her face was

hot from the heat and embarrassment. From the anger. She was mad at herself and at Mr. Hack. She was mad at Mr. Melvin for dangling the carrot, dragging her along. She took a more direct approach. "Mr. Melvin, you've told me you were innocent. I've said that I believe you. I'm reading your memoirs. So why not help me get this out, make things right?"

The first hint of a smile found the old man's face. Only it wasn't a nice, grandfatherly smile, but a sly, prison-yard grin that creased the folds in his face and narrowed his eyes. "Make things right, that what you said?"

Nita fought to hold his stare. "Well yes, I mean, I can understand how—"

Mr. Melvin set his head back and suddenly the temperature in the room dropped a few degrees. "Fifty years and now you're going to fix it? Oh, to be young and dumb again."

The way he said it made her feel small, like a little girl. Fine, Nita thought. She'd had enough. She gathered her things, got to her feet. She was all set to give the old man a piece of her mind and make a grand exit when the local news returned with a breaking story.

The ticker scrolled, *Protestors clash with Demonstrators.*

Nita forgot about leaving. She half-stood and half-sat as the screams and cries filled the room. The news flashed to some sort of march or riot, it was hard to tell. Over the shouting, a reporter spoke about the two sides. Of hate and nationalists and counter demonstrations. The shot panned the landmarks and only then did Nita realize what she was seeing. Not some distant, war-torn land, but right up the road in Richmond, Virginia.

Her stomach pulled at the sight of the men in hoods, hoisting Confederate battle flags. Nita winced, her eyes fell to her arms, to her brown skin now covered with bumps, to her useless, trembling hands. She blinked, fumbled with the recorder, the red light on, picking up her own sharp gasp and then the wet, jagged breath that escaped her throat.

When she managed a glance to her left, she found a new set of eyes fixed to her. Mr. Melvin's gaze had sharpened, narrowed until she felt him studying her thoughts. She blinked, caught her breath and looked around wildly, like a person who'd collapsed hours ago and was now regaining consciousness.

Again Nita reached for her things, a slight quiver in her voice. "Well, maybe I should..."

Another scream on television stopped her cold. The screen split from the reporter and replayed the violence at Monument Avenue. The trash and debris strewn across the wet streets—streets clogged with overturned benches and shattered glass. People scaling the monuments, teeth gnashed, faces flushed, shouting at those kicking and shoving beneath them. A girl clutched her head, another man held a towel to his bloody face. Tear gas hung over the city like smoke over a battle, as a few helpless beings lay like lumps on the pavement. A man spat at a statue. Another man hurled a brick at him.

Nita fought to hide the terror flooding through her body. Again, she felt Mr. Melvin was reading her, same as she was reading his memoirs. She turned again to the guitar, a hollow ghost in the shadows. The old man's voice was low, like distant thunder after a storm. "See what you're up against, Nita?"

She hadn't realized Mr. Melvin had risen from his seat until he turned off the television. Nita swallowed down the sawdust in her throat. Every muscle in her body was coiled tight. "No. What's happening?"

"Are you scared?" he asked, and Nita blinked.

They stood in the room, the door open and begging her to walk out. Nita managed a nod, her voice slow to catch up. "Yes."

"Okay." He nodded. "That's okay. Use it." The anger in his voice had changed. Like he was angry *for* her not *at* her now.

His jaw was clenched, his brow heavy. He stared at the blank TV.

After a minute he shook his head. Spat out some curse words. "You know, seeing that happening again... seeing through your eyes just then..." He paced about, shaking his fists, hands balled tight into blocks. Fists covered with scars, fists that looked like they'd punched through concrete. He fought with something in his head before he stopped to catch his breath. He turned to Nita. "Look, I'm sorry about what I said earlier. You see..."

Another coughing fit stole his breath without warning. Nita stood in the room, waiting him out, flinching with each cough, rattled to the ribs because the violence was still fresh in her mind. The violence her neighbor had been trying to hide from her.

The coughing took the life out of him. When he finished he looked thinner, his eyes were reddened, his chest sunken. He took a deep breath. "Enough for tonight. Come back and we'll talk. I promise."

That would have to do. Nita started for the hallway but stopped. She turned and held the recorder out—light still on—and positioned the microphone towards the old man. "No more games? You'll answer questions?" She held fast to what was left of her composure. She kept her eyes fixed on his and smiled in a noncommittal way, the way she'd seen Ingrid Houston smile on TV.

He straightened himself, wiping his chin with his handkerchief. Nita couldn't help but see spots of blood. Her smile vanished.

"Mr. Melvin are you okay?"

"You have my word."

# CHAPTER 9

At home, Nita locked up tight and double checked the locks on the windows. She rubbed her arms, having gotten used to the warmth next door. She fell into the couch and stared at the ceiling until her heart stopped leaping around in her chest. Then she flipped on the evening news.

More spitting. More screaming. More anger and more smoke. While Nita knew being a journalist meant she'd have to toughen up, it didn't mean she had to sit through all the hatred bleeding into her living room. She turned the TV off and opened a book instead.

The words on the page were no match for the images in her head. The echoes of the screams. The chants. The marching. She closed the book. Then she saw the recorder sitting on the table.

She pressed play and there it was. The news. Her fears. His fears. The coughing and the sound of her voice she hated so much. She listened again to the anger in the old man's voice. The terror in her own reaction. The hiss of the silence between them as they stood in his living room. The chills returned to her arms.

Nita picked up the third notebook.

*One day, Mary and I went out to have a picnic. We took to our secret place up near the Peaks of Otter, where we always liked to drive up during the week when less people came around. We sat on the rocks, near the creek under the sprawling trees, free to be ourselves for a while. But Mary was acting awfully strange, wringing her hands together, her eyes darting around. She couldn't sit still.*

*When she finally came out with it and told me, she was erupting with happiness. She gushed. Joy sprang from every beat in her heart. Then she saw my face and all her joy vanished.*

*Something broke inside of me. It ripped my insides out. And as I stumbled towards the tree line, falling to my knees and releasing my insides, I hated myself for it. For the snap of fear. Terror. It should have been a joyous occasion but instead it was a nightmare.*

*A baby meant the end, not the beginning.*

*But Mary wouldn't hear it. She didn't understand. And that hurt, too, but it also made me angry. I wanted to hold her and tell her everything was okay. But I couldn't. I could only pound my fist until my knuckles bled. It was all a lie. All we'd know was trouble. Trouble she couldn't fathom. She had no idea what was coming for our baby—or for me, or what was coming her way afterwards. Of course, I knew. I knew once a baby came out to the world, our secret was told.*

*That baby was a confession. It was simple as that.*

*I tried to explain, but she wouldn't listen. She didn't care if her white skin would lose its luster once she gave birth to my child. Nothing but terror awaited that baby.*

*I started looking at trees a little closer, wondering which branch would hold still for my death when they strung me up to dangle.*

*Mary listened to Bob Dylan. She thought times were changing. They weren't, not fast enough, anyway. Sure, Mary knew we couldn't be seen together but afterwards she was free. I was never free. I was never free from the stares on the sidewalk, never free of the chance encounter with the sheriff at night. Never free from the fact that I was one accusation away from being dead. Only a whisper ahead of terror.*

Nita closed the notebook. Sometimes she could read a book in a single night. But these stories were too much. They had to be paced out, soaked in, absorbed slowly, page by page. Nita needed her stamina to read such pain. In fact, she hadn't known she was crying until a tear hit her lap.

It was late when she heard the lock turning. Her mother apologized for the new hours but explained how it would be nice to have a little extra money to spend. She asked if Nita had heard anything else about the market. The market. Right down the street. She'd been fifty years in the past.

Nita shook her head. "So, this overtime, are you working nights now?"

Her mother shrugged, fanning her face and complaining about the heat as she went to the fridge for the pitcher of tea that had sat in the back of the fridge for a week. She took a sip and grimaced.

"Some. They said it's only temporary. I don't have a choice really."

Nita closed her eyes. She must have looked down after reading what she'd read. She tried to smile. "I know."

"Come here, sweetie."

Nita's mother took her in her arms. Nita closed her eyes,

breathed in the smell of sweat and vanilla and desperation. Nita used to tell herself once when she became a bigtime journalist she would do all she could to help her mother out. Now she shuddered at the thought. She couldn't even help herself.

Her mother sighed. "I'm sorry it has to be this way, but hey, I'll get caught up on bills, maybe you and I can go out sometime, right?"

Nita set her head against her mother's chest. She enjoyed the warmth of her arms, the touch of her hand on her back, the willful beat of her heart against her ear. Sometimes it was easier to be a little girl.

Nita's mother sighed. "So, what did you do this evening?"

With her mother's chin on her head, Nita was lost in thought. "Well, I went over to Mr. Melvin's and..."

Chin gone. Hand gone. Heartbeat racing. Nita's hand rose to her mouth, but it was too late. The moment vanished as Nita's mother pushed her away, eyes bugging, her warmth turning hot with rage. Her voice low but stern.

"Nita, tell me you did not go over there." Her mother's eyebrows arched. "Inside?"

Nita's mother paced. She cut a path to the kitchen and back. Then another one. Her mouth snapped shut. She wiped back her hair. She shook her head. Nita took a step back, into a dining room chair. Her mother grabbed her arm. Nita jerked away.

"Nita."

"Yes, I did. For an interview," she said, adding, "We left the door open."

Her mother's eyes flashed. The edge returned to her voice. "Nita, what are you thinking? You know that man is not right. You know what *he did*, don't you?"

Not right? What was that supposed to mean? Besides, would she rather Nita sit alone in an empty apartment? Talking to herself? Had she seen the news? The protests? The rioting?

Nita took a breath. She wanted to defend Mr. Melvin, but she also knew to be careful. "He's fine, Mom. In fact, I think there's more to his story than we know."

Her mother dumped the tea into the sink. Drops splashed on the curtain, on the counter. Even to the floor. Her mother sighed like it was Nita's fault. It was always Nita's fault. "More than we want to know, Nita."

She rinsed the sink. She picked up a pan. After a full minute of furious scrubbing, she set the pan down and turned halfway around but stopped. "Nita. You listen to me and listen good. You will not go back over there, you got that?"

Nita wanted to protest but her mother's eyes carried the warning. This was not a debate. Nita took a breath big enough for the two of them. "Fine."

Her mother went on about responsibility but eventually lost steam. Nita could tell she was tired, and she got back to the scrubbing. Not so furiously, but miserably. Nita cursed her own big fat mouth. She wanted to be back in her mother's arms, to hug her and tell her she loved her. But she couldn't force herself to walk across the room and say the words, knowing she'd just lied to her face.

Because Nita was going back to Mr. Melvin's house. She already knew that much.

# CHAPTER 10

O n the bus, Nita sat slumped against the window, seeing everything and nothing at all. A blur of green, quick bursts of new life. Spring was blooming, and she should have been excited after her big chance with Mr. Melvin. But after her lying, the fight with her mother, the news—it all hung heavy on her head. And there was the whole thing with Earnest.

Once again, he wasn't on the bus. Nita hoped it didn't have to do with the way she'd blown him off. With the warmer weather, he could've been on his bike, making his dumpster rounds before school, but looking to the empty seat across from her, Nita sure could've used some company.

Why had she let something Tamika said come between them? Why wasn't she strong enough to stand up for her friend? Why had she turned her back on him the other day?

The rest of the bus swirled with nonsense about what had happened at the market. Everyone had a different version of the story: Mr. K had an Uzi. He was in the mafia and some guys had come to collect. The store had been robbed by police and the whole thing was staged. Nita rolled her eyes. If they believed half of what was being said, she had a sinkhole to sell them.

The national news wasn't any better. More fighting in the streets. More riots at the monuments. Men with helmets and flags and more tear gas and fires. It was like her own country, right down to the ground she walked on, wasn't real at all. Like she'd woken up and found the world she knew had been yanked out from under her feet.

Nita needed to talk. And she knew her favorite teacher didn't have a class fifth period. She slunk down the hall, and arriving in the room, Mrs. Womack took one look at her and said she would write a pass.

Shutting her door, Mrs. Womack pointed to a desk in the front row. Nita sat carefully, hoping someone had cleaned it because Bryan Tillman sat there and Nita had seen him slobbering as he slept through class. And not only did he drool like a leaky faucet, but he had the worst gas of any boy she'd ever met.

Mrs. Womack perched herself at the edge of her desk, her blue shirt shimmering under the overhead lights. Mrs. Womack always looked so put together. You'd never know she'd been lugging a baby around in her belly last fall.

A baby. A shiver ran down Nita's spine. Had Mary Werrins given birth to a confession?

Nita rubbed her neck. She shifted and Mrs. Womack arranged some books in a neat stack on her desk. Nita relaxed some, her fears melting. She loved Mrs. Womack's classroom. She loved the discussions, the knowledge, the possibilities of what her favorite teacher might lay out before her.

"I like your shoes," Nita said, smiling at her teacher's shiny blue heels. Mrs. Womack smiled back. She stuck one shoe out and craned her neck.

"Oh, well thanks, Nita. You know it took me a while to get

back into these things after the baby and all. It's nice being able to wear normal clothes again."

"I thought you were pretty when you were pregnant."

Mrs. Womack tapped the shoe on the floor, raising an eyebrow. "Are you after another extension?"

They laughed, and for Nita it was nice to laugh considering the way her day was going. She looked out the window, at how the sun washed a golden light over the elementary school across the parking lot. Nita missed those carefree days of art and recess.

Mrs. Womack followed her gaze. "Everything okay, Nita?"

Nita sighed. "I was watching the news last night. Why are people acting like this?"

Mrs. Womack closed her eyes. A small shake of the head as she set a book in place. "I take it you mean the riots in Richmond?"

Nita nodded.

"The short answer? Fear."

Like Earl Melvin had said. But the images kept replaying in Nita's head. She saw the destruction, the two sides colliding. The teeth gritting, the kicking and punching. She blinked the images away. "Okay, but if everyone is scared, I mean, you'd think that... I mean, if both sides are scared, who's winning?"

Mrs. Womack's shoulders took a ride with her sigh. "I wish I had an answer for you, Nita. To be honest, when all of this started, I thought, you know, sometimes it can be good to hash out our differences. To work things out. Most of us thought things would blow over. But that doesn't seem to be the case. Fear spreads hatred. And there's a lot of fear out there right now."

Nita had always liked the way Mrs. Womack spoke to her. How she trusted Nita could handle adult topics. But lately, with the news, Nita almost wanted her to lie.

Nita picked at the spirals on the notebook, tried to keep her voice low, measured. No big deal and all. "Well, this story I'm doing—might be doing. It's, I don't know, if things keep going like this…" Nita's attempts at composure sputtered to an end.

Mrs. Womack smiled. "Are you ready to divulge some information about this assignment?"

Nita bit her smile, shook her head.

Mrs. Womack stepped closer. "I didn't think so. Look, Nita. I know you're nervous. About what's happening. Trust me, having just brought a baby into this world, I worry too. But you have to believe, *we* have to believe that, you know, good will prevail. And as for your story, my girl, you have to trust yourself."

"That's not so easy," Nita mumbled.

"Look. I'm guessing you're also feeling anxious after… your last assignment. But think about this, nothing great comes from quitting. Every writer has experienced what you're going through right now, okay?"

Nita looked up. "Really?"

"Yes. So put it behind you. Learn from your mistakes and trust yourself to do the right thing. Trust your instincts to guide you through. Trust that good will win in the end."

Nita chewed on this. She almost always took advice from Mrs. Womack—who Nita could say with near certainty was someone who did not talk to herself.

The vents rattled along from under the window, ticking and clicking like the thoughts skipping through Nita's head. She was still nervous about the news. And about taking on something as big as Mr. Melvin's story. About her mother. Everything. But now she was bolstered, planted deep like flag post ready to bear the heavy winds. And with those winds at her back, Nita found herself getting up from Bryan Tillman's desk and launching into her teacher for a hug.

"Oh."

Nita squeezed her tight and then let go. Mrs. Womack's smile shined, her eyes big and sincere. Nita looked down at the floor. "Sorry, I, I don't know why... I just..."

Mrs. Womack said it was perfectly okay. She said maybe if there were more hugs in the world things might be different.

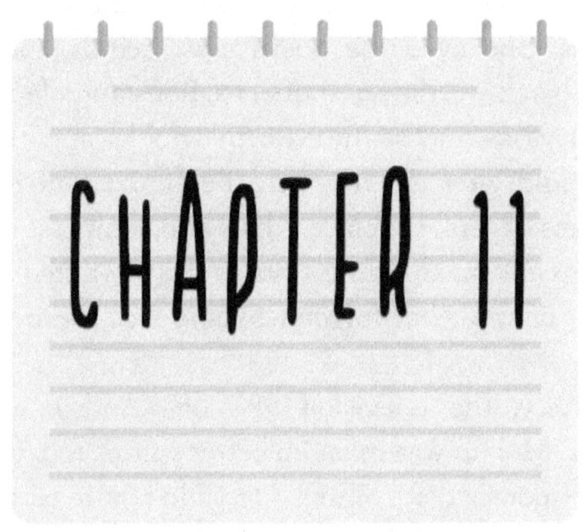


Nita arrived home to another note. Her mother would be home around ten, dinner was on the stove. The note was clear, especially the stern warning in all capital letters with four exclamation marks about going next door. But Nita, who never liked to lie to her mother, knew this was a special circumstance. One involving history, injustice, and yes, quite possibly, a Pulitzer Prize.

And after reading volume three, how could she not go?

Five minutes later, Nita knocked on his door, recorder in hand, shifting from one foot to the other, her mother's note and all those exclamation marks balled up in her pocket.

Right up until the other day, Nita thought for sure the old man lived in a dark, cave-like room that stunk of pipe smoke and moth balls. Now, for the second time in two days, she walked into the warm, sunlit refuge, thinking just how wrong she'd been.

Mr. Melvin started to set the book at the door, but Nita had already brushed past him, wandering across the polished floors to the built-in shelves lined top to bottom with wonder.

Her lips parted as she closed in on the old black and white photographs. She eyed the books and records, the exquisite carvings of black warriors and queens, lions and elephants. She studied the vases and sculptures, the masks and the colorful birds he would later tell her were Bee-Eater and Kingfishers. The old maps of faraway places, dials and compasses, and these shaker things and small drums Nita so badly wanted to touch. It wasn't long before Nita forgot why she was there in the first place.

Thankfully, the television was off. And now that she noticed, Mr. Melvin was in much better spirits, today, humming along as he polished furniture. He didn't huff or grumble or even seem to mind Nita roaming the room, taking in the pictures, asking questions about the faces. Rosa Parks, Jackie Robinson, Nat King Cole. Mr. Hack thought feigning interest might lower the old man's guard, but Nita's interest was genuine, and somehow, in the process, the old man had placed a rag in her hands. Before she knew it, she was doing most of the polishing.

Nita came across a boxer on the wall. "Who's that?"

"That, is Muhammad Ali. Here help me move these chairs."

Nita peeled herself away from the rows and rows of pictures. Hack instructed Nita to get cracking. Nita got herself back on track. Without asking, she hit the red button on her digital recorder and got to work. "Mr. Melvin, did you ever think about running away with Mary?"

The old man dropped his old cloth. He shot Nita a look. "Just coming right out with it tonight, aren't we?"

"You don't have to answer the question."

*Come on, kid. Chin up.*

Nita looked to the windows. While her apartment was furnished with cheap, dingy blinds that were bent and broken in places, Mr. Melvin's windows held honey wood shutters with thick, moveable slats that played tricks with the sunlight. The old man grunted as he got to his feet, his knees popping like bubble wrap.

He motioned to another chair. "Here, have a seat."

Nita did as she was told. Mr. Melvin wiped his brow. His old hands were like big, cracked baseball mitts. "Of course, Nita. I thought about leaving with her. So many times. In fact, sometimes I still think about it."

Nita's chest fluttered. "Really?"

Mr. Melvin nodded. "She begged me to, but it wasn't so simple."

"Why not? Where would you have gone?"

"I don't know. North. Maybe Canada. Seemed like there had to be a place where we could be together... but..."

"But if you had..."

"Well, if I had, maybe this story would have turned out differently." Mr. Melvin chuckled. He closed his eyes, the years reeling back in his head as his face relaxed in the sunlight. "The first time she smiled at me. Really smiled at me. Well, we were alone, in the back, I'd been sent up to help her clean up the stockroom."

Mr. Melvin paused and bore into the wall with his eyes, his voice going soft. "She had this way of talking to you... made you feel special. I'd seen her with the porters and orderlies, she treated us the same she did those doctors and patients. Ah, sweet Mary."

Nita gave him a minute to savor the memory, even as Mr. Hack kept chiming in with his usual poor taste for timing. A good journalist knew when to press and when to pull back. And sure enough, Mr. Melvin emerged from his thoughts with a smile. He had a nice smile, Nita thought, even if his face was rougher than a pair of summer feet.

He stood and hobbled over to a shelf, slipped out a shiny

record from a faded cover with the face of a dark-skinned woman. Mr. Melvin set the record on what Nita had thought was a sewing machine but turned out to be a record player. He set the needle down to some crackling.

*I put a spell on you.*

Nita froze. It was eerie and enchanting all the same. Tangled in the song's melody, a voice in the speakers sent an electric wiggle all the way down her scalp to her neck and down her back. Again, Nita forgot all about the interview. "Who is that?"

Mr. Melvin sat down, slung his rag against his foot and smiled. "Nita Simmons, meet Nina Simone."

*Because you're mine.*

Nita felt the voice pulling at her, worming into her ear and grabbing her from the insides then wringing her out again. She felt it in her arms, her legs, clutching her bones with such strength that all she could do was close her eyes and listen. It was the richest voice Nita had ever heard, filling the room with an almost creepy presence. When Nita finally remembered to breathe, it was a gasp.

"You like it?" Mr. Melvin asked with surprise. "Most kids your age listen to garbage, so for you to appreciate Nina says a lot about you, kid."

Even with the door cracked, the old man kept the radiators broiling hot in his place. But the song sent chills down Nita's back. The melody left her arms and legs puckered with chicken skin. Nita shook her head. "She's incredible."

The old man chuckled.

*Mayday, mayday, Nita, this is your professionalism calling. Stay focused...*

Nita cleared her throat. She blinked her eyes and tried to drown out both Mr. Hack and the beautiful singing voice in the room. She was kind of hoping her recorder was catching the music.

She shifted in her chair. "Mr. Melvin, um, you were saying about Mary, how she treated everyone fairly. But when did things move from, um, friendship to something..." Nita paused to choose her wording. "Something else?"

Mr. Melvin snapped out of whatever little moment he was having. His eyes opened and the smile that had creased his lips tightened into a straight, irritable, scowl. Then he began.

"Well Nita, there were a lot of nights when it was just the two of us. Mary would complain how her daddy wasn't a nice man, which, I found out for myself later on. Her momma was sick and her family needed her around to care for her. Oh, but sometimes we'd drive. And sometimes we'd listen to music. She loved Nina Simone. Let's see, back then I was also listening to Sam Cooke and following what was happening in Washington with the movement and..."

"What year was this?"

"Oh, um, '64, I suppose."

Nita wrote down what she could as Mr. Melvin dove back in. "I don't know, but there was something, I mean, despite our obvious differences we had a lot in common. We were both twenty-three, almost twenty-four. Our birthdays were only three days apart....and..."

Nita noticed a spark in the old man's eyes as he spoke about Mary, one that clouded over when he returned from the trip. She felt the pain in his voice, and she almost felt bad for making him talk about something so terrible. For a while the crackle of the music was the only sound in the room. The powerful voice crooned over the old speakers.

*I put a spell on you...*

"Mr. Melvin?"

The old man sat, eyes closed again, fading, until a clash of horns beeped outside and snapped him back. A switch flipped. Mr. Melvin went from great orator to grumpy old man. "Well Nita, to answer your original question, I guess we just fell in love."

# CHAPTER 12

*A*nd that, *my student, is what we in the biz call, the details...*

Back in her apartment, Nita rubbed her arms, missing the warmth from next door. The ceiling thumped with the beat of music from passing traffic. She switched on the lights and looked around at the shabby walls with scattered decorations, crooked oriental fans, and the plastic gold framed picture that had been on the wall since as long as she could remember. She reached out to straighten them then left her palm set against the wall. It was hard to believe the other side was so full of life and history.

"It didn't feel so great. It felt... awful."

*Awful? Nita, you're going to blow this thing wide open. Forbidden love... wrongly accused... an innocent man in jail for twenty years! Nita come on, this is our big chance!*

"Let me ask you something," Nita said, talking loudly, pacing. She spun back around, her hand planted on her hip. "Is that all you think about? The story?" She threw her hands up, pointed at the wall. "And what about that broken-hearted man over there, huh? What about him?"

*Now take it easy, kid. No need to go cracking up on me, hear?*

Nita fell onto the couch. She dug in the cushions for the remote control. "I can't do this. Even if it's all true. I can't break this story. All this stuff about race and love and what if... I don't know, everything on TV. I don't want this anymore... it's too..."

*Oh, that's the spirit, Nita. Just give up because you're afraid. You're scared, that's all, nothing more than a scared little girl—*

"Shut up."

Zap. Hack was gone. Nita took a breath and her stomach growled. She gave up on the remote and put together a peanut butter sandwich. The bread was hard but nothing a few seconds in the microwave couldn't fix. She waited for Hack to return but he never did. With some food in her stomach her mind regained its charge.

She picked up the notebook and forced herself to read about Mary Werrins and her baby. Mr. Melvin's baby.

*I couldn't do it. No way could we bring a life into the world this way. We would have no chance. Mary dreamed of Canada, like it was some fairyland. But I couldn't do it. I was too afraid. But deep down I knew it wasn't anger, but fear holding me back. And Mary saw the fear in my eyes.*

*That's what hurt the most...*

Nita thought about fear and anger and what her teacher had said. She thought about Mr. Melvin's fears. Her own fears. Her mother's fears. The fear on television. How fear became anger and paralyzed people. How it seemed to happen again and again and again.

She made notes. She made plans. She stopped after a few sentences, waiting for Hack's pesky voice but only hearing the hum of her quiet apartment. She got back to the third installment. Only one notebook to go after that. And the more Nita read the less she wanted to finish.

But she pressed on. She read until her eye watered with exhaustion, until the blinking became closing. She woke to her mother tapping her on the foot. "Nita."

"Huh?" Nita moaned, rolling over to the other side of the couch.

"Let's get you to bed."

Nita rubbed her eyes, still swimming in a fog of sleep and history. The moon shined through the curtains on her mother as she stood over her with ragged breaths, heavy and warm as they fell over Nita's face. Nita blinked. "What time is it?"

"It's late, after eleven," she said. As Nita's eyes adjusted, she saw her mother's glance fall to the book. Nita held it closer to her chest.

"What are you reading, anyway?"

Nita sat up on her elbows. She pulled the notebook close, protecting her lies. "Just some notes."

"Notes, huh? You know what, never mind. We'll talk in the morning. I'm beat."

Even half-asleep Nita felt the sting of her lies. The pain in those pages. The remorse and the sadness anchoring each word made them heavy in her arms. She knew she wouldn't talk to her mother in the morning, even though she knew she was going to have to come clean at some point. But her mother would be sleeping or working or somewhere in between.

Nita wandered back to her bed in a daze. Her head hit the pillow. She was out before she could get under the covers.

# CHAPTER 13

Another day without Earnest. Nita spent her morning at the bus stop listening to three boys argue over a basketball game. At school, she found Tamika waiting by her locker, which would have been nice but Nita was in a hurry to get to the library and squeeze in some writing time.

Tamika gave Nita a playful shove. "So, I just wanted to say that even though you mumble to yourself and live in the library, I'd still like to hang out once in a while."

A smile tugged on Nita's lips. She set the notebook in her locker for safe-keeping. "Are you sure, I mean, what about all your new friends?"

Tamika fell back, her shoulders slouching. "What? Oh, no. This isn't about me. You're the one always 'working on a story.' But it's cool, when you're a famous reporter and I'm a famous singer, I'll grant you an exclusive interview."

Nita rolled her eyes. "Oh thanks."

"It's true," Tamika said as Nita shut her locker and they started down the hall. "When I get discovered, I'll be switching schools, or who knows, maybe I'll have to hire a private tutor. One who can fly on my jet and teach me fractions."

"I hope it's a long flight."

"Shut up!"

Tamika's laugh made Nita laugh, and for a moment she missed the carefree days of their friendship. But she had too much on her mind to miss it too much. The words were coming now, she could feel it. Now she needed to decide once and for all if she was really going through with this.

"Well, I'll see you at lunch." Tamika smirked. "That is, if you're not eating with your boyfriend."

Nita rolled her eyes, about to tell Tamika off when her friend spun away, wagging a finger at her. "You can deny it all you want, but I know you like him."

The sun was in the wrong place when Nita arrived home. She'd lost track of time in the library, telling herself she was doing research but instead searching for a way to bring the story from then to now.

Roaming the empty hallways, in the solitude of empty classrooms, between the rows of shut lockers and the smooth, gleaming floors sliding beneath her soles, Nita took inventory of her troubles. All the lying to her mother, the thing with Earnest, Tamika, and yes, still, the retraction. But even with all the present-day problems keeping her mind busy, she kept coming back to the biggest question on her mind these days: what happened to Mary Werrins?

She walked the two miles home in a daze, without seeing much of the world around her, still stuck on that last lingering question. Oh, the questions Nita had for Mary. A face-to-face, a phone interview, even contact by email, would be gold. By the time she got home, climbing the porch and into the foyer, she heard the lively jazz music leaking from her neighbor's apartment.

Nita was drawn to his door. She knocked twice, then took a breath and laughed at herself for the flush of nerves in her chest. She smiled at how loud he had the jumpy music blaring. Then she caught a waft of something savory. Was he cooking in there?

The door swung open. "Nita, come in."

Mr. Melvin's voice was without its usual growl. Nita found her friend light and easy, wearing an apron no less. He turned, whistling as he drifted through the apartment, dancing along with the song crackling from the speakers.

Nita's eyes brightened, seeing him so nimble, quick on his feet, looking like a man who'd jumped into his pants with both legs at the same time.

"So where have you been?" he asked, wiping his hands.

Nita got the feeling he'd been expecting her. "Oh, just wandering."

The old man nodded, as though he understood. Nita shut the door without a thought. She let her bag slip to the floor and traipsed around the room, once again drawn to the faces in the frames. "So, what are we listening to today?"

"This, my dear, is the great John Coltrane."

Like Muhammad Ali, Nita had heard of John Coltrane, but never *heard* him. The music was fast and zippy, something Mr. Hack would like for sure. But Nita didn't dwell on the music for long. Nearing the kitchen, her stomach started sending messages. She closed her eyes and smiled. "Something smells delicious."

Mr. Melvin leaned his head back over his shoulder, and Nita swore the old man was moving like a kid, or at least twenty years younger. "Just my world-famous pork chops," he said between hums and snaps.

Nita closed her eyes. She felt like a cartoon character whose feet rose off the floor as the scent picked them up by the nose and led them to the meal. She peeked in where Mr. Melvin had two slabs of meat sizzling on a skillet. Two pieces.

"Are you hungry?" He cut his eyes towards Nita. She gave him a big, hopeful smile. Mr. Melvin laughed. "I'll take that as a yes."

The two neighbors took their places at the table. Everything shined under the lights after their cleaning sessions, and on the table sat shining brass candle holders, catching Nita's reflection under a flickering flame.

To go with the pork chops were sides of green beans, scalloped potatoes, and even rolls. Butter too. Nita licked her lips. A meal like this didn't happen too often next door.

Mr. Melvin held up a beer bottle. "To our health."

"Cheers." Nita clinked his bottle with a glass of ice water.

Whatever people said about the old man, they sure couldn't call him a bad cook. Being used to peanut butter sandwiches, Nita stuffed her face. Mr. Melvin was in a great mood and the music was fun and the pork chops were delicious.

When he asked how she was doing, Nita sighed. Between the meal and the hypnotic saxophone melody, her belly was full and her guard was down.

"Oh, I'm fine, well, you know..."

"No, not really I don't. Been a long time since school for an old coot like me."

Nita eyed the man carefully across the table, over the remains of the nice dinner he'd made. She thought about her mother and she set her fork down, sat back and placed her hands on her stomach. "Well, things aren't great, that's for sure. You know, I had my last assignment retracted from the paper." Nita popped herself on the forehead with her palm. "I completely blew a story, and, not only that, I didn't know when to cut my losses and give up and so I made a complete fool out of myself."

"Well, you are persistent. I'll grant you that."

She sat up, shook her head, feeling the pressure being released with each word. "It was terrible. I just knew something was going on, being covered up, and I wanted to get the truth out. But in the end," she sighed, "it was maintenance all along. And I'd dug my own sinkhole."

Mr. Melvin wiped his face. "I'm not sure I follow, but—"

"Now everyone at school is laughing at me, and my teacher, who for some reason thinks I still have credibility, granted me an extension. But she could extend it until next year because I can't write for squat. Not only that, I turned my back on my best friend, Earnest—I think you know him—and to top things off, I can't even pay my dues or come up with a decent sentence for my essay. Oh, and there's Mr. Hack, who's mad at me for—"

"Whoa now, Nita. Now slow down some."

Nita caught her breath. She looked to her plate. "Sorry."

Mr. Melvin took a bite, chewed, sipped his beer and then wiped his face. "So, you had some trouble with a story. You said, a retraction?"

Nita nodded. She stole the last roll. "Yeah, and now everyone thinks I'm a fraud."

"Like, fake news?"

Nita casted a glare that seared the old man's pork chop. He held up his hands, "Okay, sorry. Couldn't resist."

"Well, yeah, they make fun of me in the hallways. Even the principal treats me differently now, and Earnest, the only one who stood by me this whole time, well, I sort of turned my back on him, literally." Nita let her arms fall to her sides. "It's confusing."

Mr. Melvin pushed around some potatoes with his bread. He sipped his beer. "I understand confusing. Confusing I know well. And I know what it's like to be judged. But you gotta stay strong, Nita. What is it they say? Never let them see you sweat."

"You sound like someone I know," Nita said. She felt bad dumping her problems on Mr. Melvin, especially after all he'd been through. She sat up in her chair and forced herself to savor the nice meal she'd just inhaled, the fun music, and the company of her neighbor.

When they finished eating, Nita cleared the table while Mr. Melvin rinsed the dishes. To her credit, she offered to help with the dishes as well, but the kitchen area was cramped, even more than her own. She stacked and carried in the plates from the table. Then she wandered into the living room, where she came across the old scuffed up guitar. Only now it had strings.

"Mr. Melvin, do you play guitar?"

"Huh?" he called back. She heard the squeak of the faucet as he turned off the water. He came around, toweling off his hands with an old brown rag, a crooked smile finding his face. "Oh, I see you found Wilma. Yeah, I used to play a little. A long time ago."

Nita knelt to closer examine the guitar. It was dinged up some but still clung to a shine. The only person Nita had ever known to play guitar was Mr. Peters, her music teacher at school. But Mr. Peters played corny campground stuff for plays and productions. Nita couldn't imagine what sort of music Mr. Melvin played.

His heavy footsteps fell in the room. "What are you smiling about?"

Nita shrugged. Because this whole time, this room, this guitar, this man, had been sitting right next door. She looked up. "You put strings on it."

Nita, losing all journalistic composure she'd ever hoped to possess, plopped down on the floor. With Mr. Melvin's urging, she set the instrument across her lap, surprised by its weight. She ran her fingers over the strings, impressed by the rich sound it produced. She looked back and found Mr. Melvin still watching, an amused look on his face.

Nita shrugged. "I don't know how to play."

The old man twisted his hands up in the towel. "Well, tell you what," he said. "If you could run this trash out to the dumpster, I'll see what I got. It's been a while."

Outside, Mr. Hack worked damage control. *Okay, eating dinner with the old timer was one thing, even all the blabbing about school and throwing me under the bus was okay. I get it, buttering him up for information, nice. But this thing with the guitar? Come on, Simmons. What gives?*

Nita had a long-standing habit of talking with her hands, something she'd worked to tame when talking to Mr. Hack. But sometimes, like now, he really got her going.

Her arms took flight. "I'm having some fun, okay? Is that so bad?"

*Fun? At a time like this? And you call yourself a journalist...*

Several eye rolls later, Nita returned to find Mr. Melvin had taken to his recliner. He had the guitar settled into his lap and he fiddled with the strings, twisting the little knobs at the end. His old shirt lay folded over at the chest, his suspenders bowed. And while Nita had never seen anyone wear suspenders in real life, she thought he wore them well enough.

Mr. Melvin shook his head and smiled. "You know, I learned to play in prison. They had these activity workshops for inmates, a few hours a week. I learned a few chords, and, well I guess you could say I took to the blues."

He chuckled, but Nita couldn't find the humor in his joke. She eyed the notebook on the table, thought about what Mr. Hack had said about the guitar. "Do you still play?"

Mr. Melvin clenched and unclenched his fist, as though getting his fingers to cooperate. "Well, I suppose it's what got me through the day, the weeks, the years and so on. Go to work, come home, play the blues. Used to play until my fingers bled, then the tips got calloused and didn't hurt so much."

He made another adjustment to the knobs. "But now it's been a while, Nita. Haven't had much reason to play at all."

Nita smiled again, because she couldn't be sure, but she thought he put those strings on there for her. Take that, Hack.

But Hack was right, the guitar had thrown her off her game. And without her pen and pad in hand, Nita felt unarmed and exposed. Then again, the old man had cooked her a nice dinner, and now, with his tongue poking out of the corner of his mouth, he was all set to entertain.

"So what kind of music do you play again?"

"None of that crap you hear today," the old man snorted, like a real curmudgeon. A few more twists and then he strummed the strings, releasing rich, powerful chords that seemed to settle his mood.

"Blues, mostly. Mississippi John Hurt, Lemon Johnson, Willie Dixon, and of course, some Robert Johnson."

"Mississippi, *what?*" Nita asked. The old man slapped the strings and chuckled. One last twist of the knob and he must have liked what he heard, nodding in agreement with each strum, like the guitar was telling him something. Then he closed his eyes and brought his foot down like a sledgehammer on the rug.

Nita jumped at the sound. Mr. Melvin hummed in tune with the stomps.

Tap...tap...tap....

Then something amazing happened, and Nita learned why the old man had named his guitar. She learned what it meant to hold fifty years of pain and hardship in between every beat of your heart. Mr. Melvin and his scuffed-up guitar came to life right in front of her eyes.

*Take this hammer and carry it to my captain, tell*
   *him I'm gone, tell him I'm gone*
*Tell him I'm gone.*
*I'm sure gone.*
*John Henry, he left his hammer, laying on the*
   *side of the road...*

His thumb and finger plucked those strings with so much force Nita thought they might snap clean off the neck. But they didn't, the beat of his foot and the wail of the strings cried out like they were dying to please him. And it was the most natural thing in the world.

When he sang, he wasn't Crawford's own criminal. Nor was he the old man next door. He wasn't even in the room. He was somewhere far away—years away—in those words of his notebooks, stomping and strumming and singing about John Henry and his hammer and the end of times.

The song carried him away. It carried Nita away. Her arms prickled, her heart picked up the beat of the man's foot slapping the floor, and it wasn't until she saw him in that song, that Nita felt the full weight of what she'd agreed to take on.

# CHAPTER 14

Nita had to force herself not to hop up and down the next day when Earnest showed up at the bus stop just seconds before the bus pulled to the curb. But she had so many questions to ask him, and even more to tell him: about Mr. Melvin and her dinner and the notebooks and the whole thing with the guitar. But Earnest never peeled away from the window.

She glanced across the aisle, looking but not looking at her friend. He wore the same muddy shoes and the same striped socks. Terrence's baggy football jersey. But something was different.

Nita was still staring, trying to figure it out as the bus neared the school when he turned to her. She tried to look away, but it was too late. His eyes caught hers.

"You know, Nita, I can always tell when you're on a story." He smiled a big sunshine smile that took Nita by surprise. "And this one must be something."

Then he was gone, his face back to the window. The bus stopped and the shuffle started. Nita tried to play cool, rolling her eyes and clamping down on her bottom lip, trying not to give herself away. Trying not to squeal.

She leaned over to the edge of her seat. "All I can say right now is that... yes, it is big. Even bigger than you think."

She sat back, feeling good about her answer. Vague but tempting. Dangle the carrot, as Mr. Hack always said. She gathered her things, thinking maybe there was hope for Earnest after all. And okay, yes, she was thinking, maybe he *was* sort of cute, in his own way. And then he bent down towards his feet and picked up an old cloudy fish tank with a crack down the side.

He hoisted it up like a trophy. "Check it out."

Okay, maybe not.

Nita spent lunch in Mrs. Womack's classroom where she began reading Notebook Four. Flipping through the must, she was thankful to be sitting in the safety of a classroom, because what she was reading took her breath away.

*When Mary didn't show up to work the next day, I knew something was wrong. Something was terribly wrong. And my fears were confirmed when her two brothers and daddy showed up later in the day. They charged right up and grabbed me, all three of them grabbed me and dragged me outside and shoved me in their truck. Then we drove.*

*They didn't drive far. And they didn't seem to care who saw, neither. We stopped at the town center, like they wanted everyone to see. Wanted to send a message, I reckon. They dragged me out to the ground and started beating and kicking me, someone fixed a noose around my neck, and I figured it was just as well. If I couldn't be with Mary, this might as well be how it was going to end.*

*The sheriff came along and saw what was happening. He took his time, but eventually Mary's daddy and her brothers were restrained and sent home. Mary's daddy called me a bunch of names before he left, nothing I'd never heard before, but there was a certain vengeance in his words when he said I'd never see Mary again. Said if the sheriff didn't do what needed to be done then they'd go see some boys they knew in the woods. Once they were gone, I looked to the sheriff, about to thank him for saving my life when he clamped my wrists in handcuffs and arrested me on the spot.*

"Nita?"

Nita jumped. Mrs. Womack shot her a look. "Oh, I didn't mean to startle you." She looked at the notebook, her head cocked to the side. "What is it you're reading there?"

Nita slapped the notebook shut. She tried to adjust her eyes —and her brain—to the room but still saw Crawford Square fifty years ago. Mrs. Womack cleared her throat, switching gears to her teacher voice. "Okay, Nita, as your editor, I think it's time you came clean with this story."

Nita took a breath. The open windows allowed a small breeze to flutter the posters on the wall. She scanned the faces above her teacher's head. Gandhi. Martin Luther King Jr. John F. Kennedy. Barack Obama.

"Mrs. Womack, have you ever heard of Nina Simone?"

Mrs. Womack's eyes widened. She made a sound Nita thought was a sneeze and hopped up with a hand on her hip, looking Nita up and down with a smirk of surprise on her face. "Nita, what do you know about Nina Simone?"

Nita thought back to that song. How the melody yanked a hold of her and wouldn't let go. How Nina Simone's voice flexed with beauty and strength, how her voice was brave and confident despite the wounds it carried. How Nina Simone seemed to use every single breath of every word to build up a sentence when she sang it.

"Do you listen to blues music?"

Mrs. Womack's maroon lipstick shined with her smile. "Well, my husband loves it. I mostly listen to gospel and jazz."

Jazz, Nita thought, thinking of John Coltrane and pork chops. Mrs. Womack shook her head. "You're full of surprises Nita," she said, still eyeing the rippled notebook under Nita's hands.

Nita studied her own fingernails, boyish things that were scuffed and uneven. But who had time to paint fingernails when there was so much work to do? She looked at Mrs. Womack. "I like her name. It's kind of like mine. But I like her voice too. My neighbor played one of her records for me. He plays guitar too."

"Oh, yeah?"

"Yeah," Nita nodded, fighting with what to say. How much to say. "He's the one." She tapped the notebook. "He's, you know, the one people are always talking about."

"Ah. Yes, I think I know who you're talking about." She lowered her eyes. "Does this have to do with Crawford's *mired legacy*?"

Nita knew she'd never live those words down. She exhaled, gave a slight nod. "Yeah. But, here's the thing. Earl Melvin?" *Here goes nothing,* she thought. "Mrs. Womack, I think he's innocent."

Mrs. Womack set her pen down. She wasn't upset, but she wasn't what one would call exuberant. "Oh. Really?"

"Uhh huh. I've been going over there, just a few times, to talk with him. Because what I'm reading here? His memoirs, as he calls them, they're pretty amazing. Anyway, that's what I want to do the story on. Only, it's awful," she added. "And I need to do some more interviews."

Mrs. Womack's smile wavered in the wake of this information. Her chestnut eyes dulled with worry. Uh oh. Nita retraced her words. "Is something wrong, Mrs. Womack?"

Her teacher shook her head and blinked a few times. "No, it's just that... Nita, does your mother know you're spending time with this man?"

*Do I* look *crazy?* Nita thought. She held her teacher's stare for one last second and then shook her head and started spilling details again. "No. My mom works late. In fact, she works all the time, now." She left out the part about lying to her mother's face, because if her mother ever found out how she'd eaten dinner with Earl Melvin the other night, her big piece wouldn't matter because she wouldn't be able to get out of bed, much less get to school.

Mrs. Womack's gaze softened. She went to speak but then closed her mouth, which wasn't at all like Mrs. Womack. Most of the time her teacher knew what to say, when to say it, and how to say it.

And again, there Nita was, standing there with her book bag. All she had to do was nod and walk, move one foot then the other. Repeat. But it all came bubbling over like water on a hot burner. About Mr. Melvin and all those things he'd done and not done.

So unprofessional, her spluttering. But Nita couldn't stop her mouth from moving. She cinched up her bag and continued to blab all about Mr. Melvin and Mary Werrins. Mr. Hack must have been asleep at the wheel, because no one said a thing to stop Nita when she started flipping through the notebook and reading passages.

About how Mr. Melvin was kicked and beaten and left to die. And when he didn't die, he was fitted for a noose. And when the sheriff did step in, it was only to haul Mr. Melvin off to jail. By then the old man's heart was broken into pieces because the woman he loved was nowhere to be found as he was charged with something awful. And so he confessed to something he didn't do, because by then he had nothing else to live for anyway.

Nita's voice broke as she described the mob descending on the jail with torches and dogs, demanding Mr. Melvin be handed over to them.

When Nita finished, Mrs. Womack shook her head back to attention, like she'd returned from wherever her mind had taken her. "Okay, dear. Um, okay, but Nita you should probably talk to your mom about it. You know?"

Nita nodded. Then she cocked her head and forced confidence into her voice. "Okay, I'm going to write about his trial. About how I think he and Mary Werrins were in love and it wasn't, you know, what everyone says."

Mrs. Womack bit her lip. She tilted her head. It wasn't like her to struggle with what she wanted to say, but it was clear she was thinking it over. Then she blew Nita's mind. "Nita," she started but her voice had left the room. She cleared her throat. "Nita, this will all need to be verified, okay?"

More nodding from Nita, but she felt her footing give way. Verified. Like a sinkhole. She knew what Mrs. Womack was thinking, that she couldn't do this. And to be honest, Nita wasn't so sure either.

Mrs. Womack stood and took a few breaths. She walked over to the window, her fingers fiddling with the buttons near the neck of her blouse. Nita followed her gaze, out to the tree line. "Nita, this... I'm not..." She exhaled. Nita looked around the room, wondering what happened. "Are you sure this is something you want to write?"

An offer made. This was her chance. A way out. And for a second, Nita started to say no, this was not something she wanted to write. Her shoulders slumped, eager to free themselves of the weight, of defeat and failure. But then, in the back of her mind, there stood Ingrid Houston, in the sand and the wind, her voice unwavering. Her reporting still clear and crisp as if she was in the studio.

Nita nodded. "It is, Mrs. Womack. I want justice for Mr. Melvin."

Her teacher took a breath. She looked at Nita long and hard. Nita stood up and held her teacher's gaze and planted her raggedy shoes on the floor. She gained her footing and Mrs. Womack gave her a nod. *The* nod.

"Very well. Go get my story, Nita."

The next morning, Nita found Earnest sitting on the front steps to her porch. He hopped up with a golf club, a new find judging by the way he inspected the peeling grip. When they started walking, Nita could tell by the way he bounced with each step that he had something on his mind. Sure enough, a few steps down the road, Earnest started talking.

"Terrence would have been eighteen today."

Nita's pace slowed. The fact that Earnest was talking about Terrence threw her off. Earnest set the club on his shoulder and went on. "He'd be graduating this year and heading to college in the fall on scholarship."

Nita nodded. Not only did Earnest idolize his brother, his dad had taken to drinking more when he'd died. No more tinkering in the garage or helping Earnest with projects. After Terrence, Mr. Calloway vanished. He still went to work and came home in the evenings, but all anyone really saw of him was a fleeting shadow in the windows. To Nita, it was like Earnest had lost a brother and a dad when Terrence died.

Nita walked close by his side. Here was Earnest opening up

and talking about the one thing he never, ever, spoke about and Nita was too hung up on her story to come up with words to say. She'd spent the whole night reading and researching until her eyes felt as though they might fall out of their sockets. By the time the bus pulled up and Nita realized what had happened, Earnest had shut down again, and it was too late to say much of anything at all.

At lunch, Nita hurried to Mrs. Womack's room with all four notebooks. She began to outline, feeling the familiar surge of adrenaline that hit when she zeroed in on a deadline. Mrs. Womack agreed to read through the memoirs. A few times Nita would peek over at Mrs. Womack and see her hand over her mouth, mumbling things teachers weren't usually permitted to say.

Google could only take Nita so far, this kind of research called for more extensive methods. After school, she scaled the steps to the Crawford City Library, where, after a quick tutorial, she worked the microfiche in the back room, her eyes squinting and her tongue in her cheek.

She zoomed through newspaper articles beginning back in June 1963. She scrolled through her town's history. The construction of the new library, the grand opening ceremony, the ribbon cutting, the closing of the public pool, and lots of articles about colored this or that—but nothing about Earl Melvin.

Finally, as Nita was about to give up, she stumbled across two scant entries in *The Richmond Times*.

One was about how the case reached the Virginia Supreme Court.

*Earl Melvin, arrested last year for the rape and assault of Mary Werrins, a 24-year-old nurse, was denied appeal yesterday. Last May, a jury took little time deliberating and returned before lunch a verdict of guilty. Mr. Melvin was sentenced to forty-five years in prison. In a bizarre turn of events, the victim had to be forcefully removed for interrupting the hearing with pleas for mercy.*

"What?" Nita's voice echoed off the walls. She stood up, chills coming over her.

The door opened, and Miss Jones peeked in. "Is everything okay?"

"Huh? Oh yes, sorry."

No. Not okay. Once she was alone again, with only the whir of the machines, Nita read the entry again, then once more to be sure. She printed both articles. How could the victim of such a horrible crime burst in and plead for mercy and be ignored? She read on, jotting down notes and names. The prosecutor was one James A. Dooley, who went on to become Virginia's Attorney General.

Mr. Melvin's public defender, from what Nita could tell, was either in over his head or didn't seem to care much one way or another about his client's fate. Nita found it odd he never put Mr. Melvin on the stand to tell his story.

She stood, curling her toes and clenching her fists. Her chills subsided as her face flashed hot. Mr. Melvin had been railroaded. But that wasn't all, in Nita's pacing and breathing and outbursts she'd missed one last tiny piece to the puzzle. She sat back down and took a closer look.

Nita had found an obituary.

*Mary Francis Werrins 27, of Crawford Virginia, passed away on Tuesday, September 4, 1968. Mary was the daughter of Nelson H. Werrins and Barbara Lynn Werrins of Amherst, Virginia. Mary worked as a nurse at Crawford Baptist*

*Hospital. She is survived by her son, Walter Clemmons Werrins.*

*The family will receive friends on...*

Nita's eyes flipped back. Mary was dead. Then she felt the blood drain from her face.

*Walter Clemmons Werrins.*

Nita blurted out, "Mr. Melvin has a son."

He had a son out there and he was busy rotting away in his apartment. Nita was up and pacing again before she knew what she was doing. "He has a son."

More fist clenching. More toe curling as her feet went numb. The room took a few spins as it sunk in. Mary Werrins was dead. Mr. Melvin had a son.

She had to see Mr. Melvin. She had to know if he'd ever met his own flesh and blood. She needed to know what had happened to Mary Werrins.

"Oh." Nita tried again to find words. Couldn't. She needed to get out of that dark room. She wiped her face, she bumped into things. She went back and found the papers she'd printed off. She thanked Miss Jones, maybe, she couldn't remember. She dashed out of the library.

Her mouth was dry. The day, the traffic, the world—all background noise. All she could hear was Mrs. Womack's words.

*Is this really something you want to write?*

Nita ran all the way home, zooming past her own door and banging away on her neighbor's. She banged and banged, as though each bang might bring an answer to her questions. After a good six or seven door-rattling wallops Nita heard him start rocking and grumbling to get up out of his chair. When he saw Nita, his irritable face fell with concern.

"Why didn't you tell me about Mary?"

He kept the confusion act going for a few more seconds before closing his eyes. "Oh."

"Yeah. Oh." Nita stood at the door, her chest heaving, waiting for some sort of explanation. Instead, Mr. Melvin shook his head.

"Nita. Again, I think we've taken this as far as we can take it."

Nita shook her head. Mr. Hack piped up.

*Nita, you can't leave. You can't just let this go.*

"Oh, I'm not letting anything go."

Mr. Melvin glanced over her shoulder, as though someone else was around. Nita shook off Mr. Hack. She thrust out the notebooks. The cover on the first one was sliding off where it had ripped. She got a grip on her anger and confusion. She took a breath and lowered her voice.

"Mr. Melvin, here's what I think. I think you brought these books outside because you *wanted* someone to know. You wanted someone to *believe* you." Her arms went up and then fell back to her sides. "Well, here I am. I've read them and I believe you. And now I've got some questions, so help me understand."

He stood in the doorway for a full minute. Nita felt her resolve weaken. She told Mr. Hack to shut it several times. She almost turned around and left when the old man looked at her, his face a wreck of conclusions as he nodded.

"Okay, Nita. Okay."

Nita blinked to keep the tears at bay. Mr. Melvin nodded at the notebooks. He opened the door wide, broke into a coughing fit, then wiped his face with a handkerchief and said, "You're right. All these years, I guess I've been wanting to tell someone about it, so..."

Nita followed him inside. The door clicked behind them. The shutters were shut tight and the dark apartment was without its usual glow. Mr. Melvin motioned for her to sit. Nita thought about her mother. She thought about her assignments, how she needed to study for math and was way behind in social studies. But this *was* social studies, she thought. It was bigger than school or anything else, really.

Nita took a seat. The old man set the notebooks down and glanced back to his room. Nita had to admit, she didn't feel much like Ingrid Houston right then. She was a bit shaky, off balance, like she had a lot to learn about things.

Mr. Melvin coughed a few more times. "It's hard though, it's still hard for me to talk about. But, there's something else you might want to see."

He hobbled out of the room, wheezing and sucking for wind with each squeaky step. Nita, still breathing hard herself, glanced around at the many faces on the wall.

When he returned, he held a handful of yellow envelopes. Nita started her recorder as he settled into his chair, because she couldn't trust herself to remember what was happening. He watched her hit the button, used to the routine but still skeptical.

"These are from her." He slapped the envelopes down on the table. They weren't actually yellow but faded, old and worn, but it wasn't until she read the neat cursive writing, *Mary Werrins, 212 Penelope Drive Crawford, Virginia*, that they became real live pulsing pieces of history.

Nita gasped, a gasp picked up by the microphone. She would hear it many times later when she listened again. The letter was addressed to *Mr. Earl Melvin, Inmate #32655, Jamesway Correctional Facility.*

She swallowed what was like sand in her throat. She looked over the postmark. The stamps. Each envelope had been sliced opened at the top. "She wrote you?"

He nodded, then—inexplicitly, Nita thought—began telling

a story. "Nita, when I was your age, I couldn't rightly skip down the street and do whatever I wanted like you kids today. We had to be aware of everything. If a white man came moseying down the sidewalk, I was supposed to scatter across to the other side. If a white woman was with him, well, I'd better scatter quietly and keep my eyes on the ground."

Nita shook her head, shaken to the core as Mr. Melvin got to his feet, the planks in the floor bending and snapping with his steps. "I couldn't eat at the counter with white folks. I had to go around back, like a dog. We had separate schools, drinking fountains, movie theaters..."

She stared at the envelopes on the coffee table. The mysterious bulge of their secrets. "Mr. Melvin—"

He held up a hand. "One summer, when I was fourteen and washing dishes at my Uncle Clyde's place, the Continental Diner, I'd just finished my shift and ducked out of my apron when a young man came back in the kitchen. A white man, college boy in a tie and oxford shirt, maybe in his mid-twenties and already bald as a baby. He was a mess, all red-faced and drunk, hollering at us for closing.

"Now, my Uncle Clyde was a great big man. But he was the nicest soul you ever met. He agreed to fix that jerk something anyway, hoping to settle him down some. But that man wanted trouble, you could see it in his eyes."

Mr. Melvin stopped hobbling around. He looked to be collecting his thoughts. But Nita couldn't take her eyes off her name: *Mary Werrins.* What was in there?

Mr. Melvin kept his eyes on Nita, his wrinkles dark and deep in the shadows as he stood. Nita couldn't tell where this was going. The way he was sweating and coughing, with yellow eyes and loose lids as he went on about some diner.

The radiator clanged to life as Mr. Melvin resumed his rounds. "No sir, he wasn't there for pancakes." His voice, always so full of strength, sounded weak and strained, as though it was shredded by time and hatred. "...that man pointed at me and said, 'What are you looking at?'

"Uncle Clyde shot me a look from the kitchen, his eyes begging me not to say anything. I guess you could say I had a problem with authority back then." Mr. Melvin chuckled—a sad chuckle—then another round of coughing. He fell into his chair. He leaned forward, so Nita could hear the tangle in his breaths.

"Well, the man asked me what I was looking at and I shrugged. That didn't make him so happy so he took a step over to where I was and asked again. He was short—I was maybe a head taller than him and knew if I wanted to I could whip him from here to Scottsboro, but Uncle Clyde told me to leave it alone."

"And then?" Nita asked, figuring she'd try to get him on track. He'd brought those envelopes out for a reason. Mr. Melvin leaned so far back she thought his chair was going to tip.

"Oh yeah, he left all right. But he came back a few nights later. This time with some friends. They called my uncle all sorts of names, Nita, names I can't say to this day. They said a black man had no business running a diner, and who did he think he was and all that mess. They cursed us and harassed us and broke up a bunch of stuff in the restaurant."

"Did you call the police?"

Mr. Melvin cut his eyes at Nita, looked at her as though she'd recited the joke of the day.

"Nita, the man I'm talking about? He went on to become our governor."

Nita clutched the arm of the couch. She wanted to protest, to argue, to... scream, maybe. But Mr. Melvin held up his hand. "Now, the reason I'm telling you this, because you can read my memoirs from here to Birmingham and back, but I need you to understand how things were, how some things still linger on to this day. This thing with Mary. You have to understand what I was up against."

He was pleading with her. For Mary. For justification. Nita sat and nodded. She understood, yes sir, she did. She was aware of what she was getting into now, and she was only more determined to get the story right. To see the contents of those envelopes.

She took a breath. She figured the letters had been screened by the prison. She wiped at her pants and tried her best to make her voice sound normal. It didn't. "Mr. Melvin, these um, envelopes," she began in a high pitched voice. Not at all like Ingrid Houston from TV. "What's in those letters?"

Mr. Melvin stared back at her, his eyes as dark as those attic windows. He shrugged. "I couldn't tell you, Nita. I've never read them."

"Wait. What? Why?" Nita blurted out the words. She couldn't help herself. She couldn't have found composure with a map and a flashlight. Mr. Melvin merely shrugged again, looking content with her bewilderment.

The old clock on the shelf ticked along. Nita's heart pounded in her ears. Mr. Melvin looked at the table, at the envelopes. "That doesn't mean I don't know what they are," he said, flipping through two of them before finding one and holding it up. "Especially this one."

"What is it?" Nita whispered.

He wiped his forehead with a rag. "Well, I'm pretty sure it's a suicide note."

Nita's lungs pulled for the air that had been sucked from the room. Mr. Melvin set one leg over the other with a grunt. Nita's lips went through the progression of forming words, but as she flipped through the thought bank of questions in her mind, the *hows* and *whys* and *whats*, nothing formed. She sat up, wiped her forehead and leaned forward to get a closer look at the envelopes. She wondered what they might contain, the contents and heartbreak and, did he say *suicide?*

It was then, in the throes of such confusion, that a locomotive rumbled down the hall and slammed into Mr. Melvin's door.

*Wham Wham Wham...*

The door rattled with violence. Nita jumped. She covered a scream—one that had already been building—with her hands. Mr. Melvin never moved.

"Nita, are you in there?"

Her mother's earth-moving voice pushed through the crack below the door. It found them in the shadows of the room. Nita contemplated a jump from the window. Twelve, maybe fifteen feet. When she turned back, Mr. Melvin stared at her with the makings of a grin.

Mr. Melvin rocked himself up and rose to his feet as another round of banging threatened to break his door down.

"Nita Simmons. So help me God if you're behind this door."

# CHAPTER 16

Nita thought the door would buckle. It was like the force of the universe was barreling down on its hinges. Her mother, having somehow acquired superhero strength, pounded three times, paused for two beats, then lay into the door again.

*Wham!*

*Wham!*

*Wham!*

Nita leaped to her feet. Mr. Melvin reached for the doorknob. He turned to her, as though to grant her a moment for any last words, but Nita had nothing. Her knees wobbled. All the fear rushing through her veins left her lightheaded.

With a chuckle, Mr. Melvin shook his head and opened the door.

Nita was almost surprised it was her mother and not say, a fire-breathing dragon. But it was her mother all right. Her eyes were wide with too much white in them. And Nita half expected her to strike her down with the point of a finger.

"What in the world is the matter?" Mr. Melvin said,

scratching his head. In the light from the hallway Nita saw how his gray hair was matted and springy.

Nita's mother did not waste time with introductions. "Nita, get your behind out here now."

Nita got her behind working. She scurried past Mr. Melvin and into the hallway. Her mother cocked her head and addressed their neighbor with a full dose of fury and vengeance. And spit. "I want you to keep away from my daughter. Do you understand me? Are we clear?"

Mr. Melvin's eyebrows went for a ride. He blinked a few times to focus, swung his glance to Nita who now stood behind her mother, somewhat ashamed considering the moment they'd shared.

*Walter!* Nita wanted to scream. *His name is Walter!*

But Nita never said a word. She turned away and let her neighbor take the fall. Mr. Melvin cleared his throat. "Miss Simmons, I can assure you that—"

Nita's mother straightened until she was almost eye level with the old man. Her whole body was tight and shaking. She seemed to be growing before Nita's eyes. Right then, Nita had little doubt she could have tied a beam of steel into a Christmas bow.

"I don't want to hear anything you have to say. All I want is for you to stay. Away. From my little girl."

Again Mr. Melvin glanced over at Nita, who cowered and looked away. Even as she wanted to stand up, make things right, her fear won out. Mr. Melvin looked at her one last time, his breaths wheezing. "Very well."

With a parting glare, Nita's mother spun off, jerking Nita by the arm. Nita took a fleeting glance at the envelopes on the table, their many secrets only moments from being told, now gone in an instant. A soft click as Melvin's door shut behind them. The click of a jail cell.

Once inside their own apartment, Nita flinched when her mother whirled around. "Talk."

And Nita, aspiring journalist, Pentip Award hopeful, said, "Huh?"

Her mother cocked her head. She thrust a hand out towards Nita. "Come on, Nita. Talk. Tell me why you won't listen to me. Tell me why you're going next door to that man's house when I specifically asked, no, I *forbade* you to do so."

Nita, only now beginning to realize she was going to live to see another day, held up her hands and took a breath. "I know, Mom, but you're going to have to trust me here."

Her mother's eyes bulged. "Trust you? Ha. *Trust you?*"

Her mother paced, and Nita knew from experience that when her mother paced her ears closed. She waved her hand, a frantic gesture, the same way Nita did when she was worked up with Mr. Hack. Then she stepped closer, demanding Nita's full attention. "Nita Simmons, you've been lying to my face and you want me to trust you?"

Nita nodded, her fear receding as her lungs filled with air again, breathing like those envelopes next door. The initial jolt of terror was fading, and now frustration was creeping into her voice. "Yes. Trust me. I'm sorry I've been lying but you never listen to me. About writing. Or how Mr. Melvin might be innocent. That he and Mary Werrins were in a relationship and he was falsely accused and imprisoned."

Nita's mother stopped pacing. "Is that what he's feeding you, Nita? He's *innocent?*" Nita's mother made a *pfft* sound. "Imagine that."

Nita yanked out the research. The papers she'd printed off. She placed them on the dinner table, sliding the bills and books to the side. "Mom, it's all right here."

Her mother didn't want to look. But Nita held firm and eventually her mother took a begrudging step towards the table when her phone dinged. She started for her pocket. Nita planted her foot and sighed. Her mother caught herself. She regarded the plea in her daughter's wet, red eyes. She ignored the phone and took a seat at the table.

"Okay, Nita, let's hear it."

Nita got to work. She explained to her mother about the memoirs. About the hospital and the budding relationship with Mary Werrins. Then about Mary's family. She even played the interviews with Mr. Melvin and then went over the sentencing and the appeals. How Mr. Melvin refused the stand. She stopped a few times, seeing something in her mother's face she couldn't ever remember seeing before. By the time she was done her mother only blinked. She flipped over the index card in her hands.

"What? Now Nita, are you sure? This is..."

Nita's mother shook her head. She didn't look angry now, or tired, or bored. Not even close. Nita closed her eyes, capturing the image. Because her mother looked proud.

"I just," Nita's mother waved the card over the table. "Nita have you done all of this on your own?"

Nita fiddled with the recorder. She looked at the laptop, the printed pages, the piles of notes, cards, and timelines. She smiled, basking in the warmth of having astonished her mother. At doing something to capture her interest.

"Yeah."

Nita thought, judging by the way her mother was looking at her, maybe now she'd fork over the money for those JJC dues. Together, they spent another full hour with the case. And that night, as her mother silenced her phone, was the best time Nita could remember having with her in a while. No complaints about money or homework. They never turned on the television. They sat at the table, mother and daughter, and pored over facts and timelines.

Every so often, Nita's mother would shake her head and look over her shoulder, back at the wall in the direction of Mr. Melvin's apartment, and she'd say, "Twenty years."

And Nita would only say, "Yeah."

That got Nita thinking. If she could convince her mother, then she could convince others. If she could really get this story right people would see for themselves what Mr. Melvin had been through. Then maybe they'd start to see how fear and anger only leads to more fear and anger. She could break the cycle.

A lofty goal. But when Nita's mother reached out and stroked her head, she knew she'd won over her toughest critic. She also knew her mother only wanted the best for her.

"Nita, you know I just worry so much about you. With work and everything, I just, I feel so bad I'm not around more."

"I know, Mom. But really, you have to trust me sometimes."

Her mother nodded. "I know baby. I'll try."

Nita stood in the kitchen, not knowing what to do with her hands, her mind, her research. "Well, I guess now I have to write this thing."

Nita had never heard someone complain as much as Earnest complained on the bus ride across town. He had a life, you know, things to do and work to be done. She owed him, he told her more than once. She owed him big.

Nita smiled. She knew all her friend needed was a little extra incentive. And she had that.

"I've got two words for you, Earnest," she said, as the bus rolled to a stop.

"Yeah, like sink hole?"

Nita's mouth opened wide with a smile. Now this was a new side to her shy friend. "Um, no. And that's one word, trust me. How about this: spring cleaning."

Earnest stopped with the leg tapping. His eyes widened as he nodded, putting it together. "Rich people spring cleaning,"

She held up her hand. "Yes, but only after I get what I need."

"Aye aye, Captain."

Two stops later the bus let them off at Brentwood. And it

wasn't long before Earnest was gawking at the massive mounds of treasures lining the curb. "How did you know?"

Nita rolled her eyes. "Give me some credit here."

His steps slowed, his eyes darted from one trash heap to the next. Then he started across the street. "Hang on, is that a...?"

"Earnest." She grabbed her friend by the wrist. "We have work to do first."

Earnest followed, his feet going in one direction and his head staring back as they walked along the wide sidewalks and wrought iron lampposts, the tidy one-way streets separated by the blooming cherry trees lining the median.

Nita's steps slowed as she studied the addresses. It felt strange, these enormous houses with copper roofs and pea gravel driveways. Her determined march staggered to a timid crawl as she reached 54 Walnut Avenue, home of Roger Dooley, son of James A. Dooley, the former state Attorney General.

Nita checked her notes. She took a breath. Two chimneys anchored a regal, two-story colonial. Shiny cars out front.

*This is it, kid. What are you waiting for? Get on up there and knock on the door.*

At her feet lay the brick walkway, lined with rows of heady boxwoods. "Just knock? What then?"

*Dive right in, kid.*

Earnest looked up. "You okay, Nita?"

Nita took a breath, nodded.

Earnest opened his mouth to speak when something across the street caught his eye. Nita followed his gaze to a pile of old windows stacked beside buckets. Some cracked planters, old fence planks, and, at the far end, a stationary bike.

Again, Nita had to restrain her friend from walking across the street. "Earnest, you promised."

He stopped and turned. "Okay," he said, "You're right." He gestured to the house with a shrug. "Well, shall we?"

Hearing him joke, Nita wished she was a happy-go-lucky boy and not a mess of nerves. But then it dawned on her how Earnest's brother was gone and his mother never left the house anymore, and then she felt bad for always dropping her problems in his lap.

"Hey E, thanks for coming along."

Earnest grinned. "Me thinks the great Nita Simmons is stalling."

Nita's shoulders drooped. She nodded. "Maybe."

Together, they approached the door. Nita tapped the brass knocker against its metal plate, careful not to bang but loud enough to be heard. On the sidewalk, two speed-walking ladies zoomed past, elbows swinging and heads nodding. Their steps slowed, but they recovered with a wave. Earnest parade-waved back.

The door opened, and Nita and Earnest were greeted by an older girl, high school age with blondish hair and a nice, oval face. She looked surprised to see them. "Hi."

"Hello," Nita said, fixing her bag over her shoulder and trying her best to compose herself. She'd been thrown off her game joking with Earnest. Hack. This girl. By the story itself. But here she was and so she'd do her best. "My name is Nita Simmons, I'm with the uh, *Crawford Chronicle.* I was wondering if a Mr. Roger Dooley lives here?"

The girl looked from Nita to Earnest, settling again on Nita with a pointed smile. "Yes, as a matter of fact he does."

Nita stammered along. "Oh."

The girl cocked her head. "You said, *The Crawford Chronicle?*"

"It's a middle school newspaper," Earnest blurted out. Right then, Nita made a note in her mind to leave him at the curb next time. She was attempting to recover when the girl called over her shoulder.

"Dad, you have a reporter here to see you." The girl turned back to them with a devilish smile. "What is this about?"

"Um, well, it's..."

The door opened wider and Nita saw the expanse of the house. A fancy, oriental runner in the foyer, the thick crown molding along the ceiling. Brass fixtures and the large, gilded frames with paintings of stern men on horseback. Then she saw an older man in a button-down shirt and khakis. Thinning gray hair, blue eyes behind wireframe glasses.

He didn't look pleased. "Ella, what are you...?"

The girl waved a hand to the door and he looked down at Nita and Earnest.

*Straighten up, kid.*

Nita straightened. The girl smiled. "This is Nita," she squinted at Nita, bit her lip, "Uh... sorry."

"Simmons."

The girl snapped her fingers. "Right. Nita Simmons. She's with the *Crawford Chronicle*."

The man's jaw clenched. "I see."

The girl pirouetted off the doorframe. "Well, I'll leave you to it."

The man stood at the door. "May I ask as to what this entails?"

Nita summoned her inner Ingrid Houston. "Yes, I'm writing a story on Earl Melvin and his trial. I'd like to ask you a few questions about your father, James A. Dooley."

The man blinked. "I see."

Nita started to slouch but caught herself. She studied her notepad. The man waited. An eternity passed. At least twenty seconds. Roger Dooley fished around in his pockets. He shuffled his feet. "Would you like to come in?"

Nita and Earnest found themselves in a sunken den, taking a seat on a plush leather couch. The room—the house, really—

felt like a time warp. The fireplace smelled of fires past. Nita took in the wood paneled walls, the paintings of soldiers in battle. Old style rifles on display. Swords. Oval portraits behind thick glass. Earnest's eyes were all over the place.

"So." Roger Dooley took a seat and pulled a tasseled loafer over his knee. Nita realized he was waiting for her to explain what she was after. He watched with interest as Nita reached for her bag and fumbled around with her pen, pad, notes, her trusty recorder, which she placed on the table between them.

"Is this okay?"

Roger Dooley nodded.

Nita pressed record. Here goes, she thought. "Your father was Mr. James A. Dooley? The prosecuting attorney at the Earl Melvin trial?"

Roger Dooley nodded again. He sat back, leaning his head against his hand, thoughtfully, with two fingers tapping his temple.

"Well," Nita said, "I've been reading what I can find about the trial. But I'm curious as to why Mr. Melvin never took the stand, why his appeal fell through. Also about Mary Werrins. Did your father ever speak about the trial? I mean, later, off the record or otherwise."

Roger Dooley shifted, his eyes never left the recorder. Nita felt like she'd dropped an avalanche on his lap but she was flustered, and Earnest wasn't helping, wiggling over there the way he was.

Mr. Dooley, now with his hand to his chin, tapped his cheek. He shifted again. "Well, Nita, to answer your question, yes. The Earl Melvin case did stick with him, if that's what you mean."

*Eureka!*

Nita bit her tongue. This was no time for talking to herself. She looked up. "How so?"

"As you probably know, my father later went on to become the state attorney general. He tried many cases, put many bad people away. Deservedly so," he added.

Of course Nita knew that. She was no rookie. Roger Dooley looked off.

*There's something here, Nita. Something he wants to say. Dig. Dig, Nita.*

"I've read that your father was proud of his trial record."

Roger Dooley cut his eyes to her. Nita breathed through her nose, slid forward on the leather couch. Mr. Dooley lowered his voice, as though hiding from the recorder. "They wanted to lynch Earl, did you know that?"

"Mr. Melvin alluded to it," Nita said, hearing the quiver in her own voice.

"So you've spoken to him?"

Earnest nodded his head towards Nita. "They're neighbors."

Nita glared at Earnest. His eyes fell to the floor. She turned back to Roger Dooley. "I have, yes."

Roger Dooley's eyes widened. He removed his glasses and set them back on his head. He regarded Nita closely, his voice catching. "So, you know him? That's very, hmm, that's quite interesting."

Nita waited.

"Nita, I think you've probably reached a conclusion here. I'm guessing you presume he was wrongfully convicted. That's why you're writing this, correct?"

Something tugged at Nita's heart. "At this point I'm only seeking the truth. I have questions about the trial, about Mary Werrins. How there was a trial without a victim coming forward. About why Mr. Melvin never testified. About why—"

"This is for a *middle school* paper?" Roger Dooley asked, incredulously, then reached for the recorder. "May I?"

Nita took a sharp breath. "Oh, okay."

He clicked the button, zapping the red light. "I'd like to go off the record."

Nita's body tingled. Earnest shifted, and for a moment the only sound was the ticking of a clock. Another glance around the den—a tribute to Old Virginia and its storied history. To the battle flags, the gray armies, the silver beards of the men watching the room. All of them were watching her.

Roger Dooley leaned forward, resting his elbows on his knees. "Nita, to your uh, other questions... well... years later, my father would often talk about the trial. Usually after a drink he'd discuss Earl Melvin with my mother, with colleagues, even with judges. He'd never seen anything like it, he said. How a man could sit there and never utter a word while his life hung in the balance. His face never cracked." Roger Dooley tapped his leg. "What was it my father used to say? Said he'd seen concrete blocks show more emotion than the man sitting on the bench."

Nita capped the pen then uncapped the pen. Now her foot was going too, tapping along because she knew more was coming. Roger Dooley took a breath, fought with something on his mind, then shook his head. He reached forward again, for the table. "You know what, my father died almost ten years ago. This should come out." He fiddled with the recorder. "How do you get it back on?"

Lightning would envy the quickness with which Nita came forward and pressed the button. Roger Dooley looked at her, then to the recorder sitting on the table like a stick of dynamite. Finally, he nodded, sat back, and continued.

"It was a hard trial. But you should keep in mind it was a different time."

Nita lost her composure. She blurted out. "But Mary never even came forward. How do you have a trial without a victim?"

Roger Dooley nodded. "Well, some said Mary was too

traumatized. Besides, they had the confession. And Nita, even those who didn't think Earl Melvin was guilty of... rape, or assault, or abducting, of all the things thrown at him, well, they still wanted him locked up. For being with someone like Mary."

"A white woman," Nita said. Roger Dooley met her eyes. He nodded.

"Yes. Anyway, when the verdict came down and Earl Melvin was found guilty, no one was surprised. It was expected, I guess. After the trial, my father came home late and went straight for a bottle of bourbon in the kitchen. Never bothered with ice, or even a glass. Only time I ever saw him do that."

Nita started jotting down words, thoughts, nothing at all. Her hand trembled, so she clasped her fingers tightly around the pen to steady herself.

"But it was at the sentencing where things got wild. Here was Earl Melvin, staring down the death penalty. And then Mary Werrins busted into the courthouse. Doors swinging—my father used to say it was like something out of a movie. How she literally threw herself at the mercy of the court. Screamed and shouted at my father, the judge, the jury who'd just convicted Earl Melvin of abducting and raping her. She said she loved him, said she'd die without him."

Nita realized her mouth was open. She shut it.

"That's when Mr. Melvin broke. Right in the courtroom. He cried and moaned and let out this inhuman roar. He started over the bannister for her and was restrained. Her family called him all sorts of names. Later they claimed he was crying over the sentencing, said he was a coward and he should be thanking God above he wasn't swinging from a tree. They said some things... well, awful things... My father said it was the worst thing he ever saw. And that's saying something."

He shifted. Nita shifted. The clock ticked. Earnest whispered, "Damn."

"Yeah, damn." Roger Dooley agreed. "But my father knew Mr. Melvin wasn't crying about his sentence, but that—"

"He was heartbroken," Nita blurted out. Roger Dooley looked at her and gave a slight nod.

"Yeah."

*Ask him, Nita. Ask him point blank.*

Nita cleared her throat. "Mr. Dooley, do you think, or, did your father think... did he think Mr. Melvin was innocent?"

Roger Dooley shifted once more, he uncrossed and re-crossed his legs. He wiped at something in his chair then looked at Nita, so deep into her eyes with his own icy blues it gave Nita a shiver.

"Yes, Nita. I think he did."

# CHAPTER 18

Nita sucked down the fresh air as they walked away from Roger Dooley's house. She did her best to perform the act, to keep her steps in a straight line, to keep her head up and her arms at her sides.

Earnest hopped around her like he was on a pogo stick. "Nita, that was... I mean, he's innocent!"

"I know," she said through gritted teeth, fighting back tears. She had to appear poised and professional until they were on the bus.

A ways down the sidewalk she gave Earnest a stern look. "Okay, here's the deal. You need to keep this under wraps. Which means when we get to my house I need to speak to Mr. Melvin. And you need to keep quiet."

After she said it, she realized she'd never envisioned a day when she'd have to tell Earnest to keep quiet. But this was a different Earnest she was dealing with. In fact, this was a day like no other.

Earnest was already headed for the trash. "Okay, okay, sheesh. So what, am I like your assistant now?"

"Something like that, yes."

Earnest smiled. "Cool. I'm happy to do whatever it takes if you're going to write this story."

Nita stopped. "Wow, really?"

So Earnest believed in her, and that meant a lot because Nita still wasn't so sure herself. But she had her mother in her corner now, and as sad as it was, Mr. Melvin's story had to be told.

Nita felt a swell of courage. A gale that almost lifted her off her feet. Something she hadn't felt since the retraction. Retraction. Whatever. She nodded again. "Yep. I'm going to get the truth out in the open. I'm going to tell Mr. Melvin's story. Earnest?"

While Nita was filling herself with courage, Earnest had procured a skateboard from the heap. He kicked off, swooshing past Nita. "That's awesome. But first, you're going to help me get this stationary bike home."

THE SKATEBOARD MADE A DECENT DOLLY, although Nita had no idea what the boy could want with a stationary bike. When she asked, Earnest launched into a detailed plan about making some sort of generator. She smiled, almost delirious. Walking out of Roger Dooley's house with all those terrible stories and now out in the open air with the sun, with Earnest and his crazy talk. The next thing she knew, she had a big goofy grin on her face she couldn't reel in. It was like her worrying had been released, like a balloon climbing into the sky.

Up the hill, things got tough. Pushing a stationary bike, tilted and not so balanced on a skateboard, took some effort. Every crack sent the bike pitching over to one side or the other. But they plodded ahead. They crossed the bridge and took the hill towards Nita's apartment. And Nita was still catching her breath from all the lugging and pushing when she reached into her pocket and realized that for all the discoveries and breakthroughs the day had brought, she'd managed to forget one important thing.

"Uh, Earnest. I don't have my house key."

Earnest never missed a beat as he waved her off. "I can get you inside, easy." He picked up the pace. Nita fought to keep the stupid stationary bike from tilting over as she tried to match his strides.

"How? I locked the keys inside."

He snorted, like keys were something used by mere mortals. He was talking more and teasing more, about the trial and everything else you could think of. When Nita asked him again how he planned on getting inside he turned and looked at her so completely Nita almost fell over with the bike.

"Give *me* some credit here, okay?"

They left the skateboard and bike on the lawn and hit the stairs. Earnest glanced at the empty rocking chair. "Is he around?"

"He's probably asleep," Nita said, knowing she still owed the old man one whale of an apology for the other evening.

Nita pushed through the main door, keeping her eyes down the hall. At the door, she wiggled the doorknob. "See? Locked."

Earnest brushed past Nita, reaching into his wallet and coming out with his library card. "Allow me."

She could tell he was enjoying playing the role of hero, as she watched him go to work. He slid the card under the doorknob, looked up to the left, squinted, and bit his lip. "All you have to do is to find the..." He straightened. "Wait, did you lock the deadbolt?"

"No, just the door handle, thingy. It locks automatically."

"I got it."

Earnest jiggled the card, his eyes shooting to the left again. He bit his lower lip, then, with a click and a twist, the door swung open. Nita found herself staring into her living room. "There you go."

Nita shot her friend a look, half impressed, half skeptical. "So, do you do this often?"

Earnest pushed his wallet into his back pocket and puffed his chest out. "I can't tell you all of my secrets."

"Like how you're going to make a generator?"

"I told you already. All I need is an alternator. A 63 amp, at least..."

Nita brushed past Earnest, shaking her head with a smile, when she heard Mr. Melvin's door squeak open. She jerked to a stop, peeked out, and there he was, staring back at her. His brow furrowed.

His lips puckered like he'd been sucking on a sour apple Jolly Rancher. He glowered at Nita, or more likely, Earnest, mumbling a few choice words under his breath as he turned around, fixing his hat on his head and huffing back towards his cave.

"Mr. Melvin, wait."

He waved Nita off without bothering to turn around. Earnest tried to hold her back but she shook him off and dashed down the hall. "Mr. Melvin." Nita caught him at the door.

He fixed his sleeves, pulling at one arm, didn't smile or even look her way. Nita took a breath, figuring she deserved as much. Why would he talk to her after the other night? After she'd used him for a story and then left him out to dry.

The old man shifted his weight and made a show of starting back inside. "I think your mama was awfully clear about this."

"Mr. Melvin, please," she said, surprising herself with the panic in her voice. He looked back to her, the mean leaving his eyes, his brow going soft. She shifted her feet. It all seemed so small now, after her talks with Roger Dooley. "I talked to my mother last night. She wants to apologize to you."

The old man let out a breath. He shifted from one foot to the other. "Yeah? I find that hard to believe."

"She was worried about me, that's all. I've convinced her though."

"Convinced her? Did you convince her you should have boys in your apartment?" He nodded at Earnest. "What would she say about that, huh? If she knew you two were in there with no one home? I bet she would skin your hide."

Nita felt heat rising to her face. "What? No, I was locked out."

*We found out the truth, Mr. Melvin. Let's do this.*

She turned back to Earnest, then to Mr. Melvin, whose face was balling up again. "Earnest helped me get in. Besides, he's not like you think." She smiled. "Like, did you know he's building a generator?" She looked back at Earnest, who'd slid back a few steps. "Or that he can fix just about anything? Probably even that old TV you're always slapping around?"

She found it hard to stop talking once she got going, adding, "And, he's here because I was locked out, walking the streets all alone. What was I supposed to do?"

Nita knew nothing frightened old people more than kids walking the streets, so she thought it was a nice touch. Mr. Melvin stared down at her, his wheezy breaths fighting through a cough. Finally, he looked back at Nita's door. Earnest popped his head back inside.

Mr. Melvin grumbled some but then said, "You said a generator?"

Nita nodded. "Yes, I just helped him drag an exercise bike across town."

"What were you kids doing across town?"

"Spring cleaning," Earnest added.

Nita glanced back at Earnest, then to her neighbor, tilting her head and using her finest nice girl voice to plead with him. "Mr. Melvin, Earnest is assisting me with this assignment. He's my, uh, kind of like my sound tech. I'd like to finish up our interviews. If that's okay, with you?"

She'd have to remember to give herself a pat on the back for such quick thinking. That speech was nothing but pure genius. Mr. Melvin looked back and forth.

"And you talked to your mama?"

Nita knew she had him then. She nodded. Earnest took a timid step out into to the hallway.

"Well, I suppose it wouldn't hurt," he said, jingling his keys. Then he turned his head and called towards Nita's door. "But if one thing goes missing, I won't be afraid to show him my pistol collection."

Nita laughed a little, looked at Earnest to assure him the old man was joking around.

Probably.

# CHAPTER 19

Inside, the lamplight gleamed off the floors, casting a cozy glow over the picture frames on the walls. Nita watched Earnest take in the room, remembering how amazed she'd been the first time she entered. Mr. Melvin, having relented to Nita's charm, never let his thick stare leave Earnest for more than a second. If nothing else, Nita thought` it was at least a start.

"Well, you coming in or not?" he said to Earnest, who still had his feet planted in the doorway. Earnest tip-toed inside, leaving the door cracked open behind him, nearly hopping out of his shirt when Mr. Melvin hobbled over and jerked the door shut.

The room felt different with the three of them. Almost cramped. Nita handed Earnest her recorder but he only fidgeted, his eyes still dancing around the room. Some sound guy, Nita thought, snatching the recorder back, thinking of all the important moments it held.

Still, Nita was grateful to have Earnest around for this day of discovery. She couldn't have done it alone. Even if it was clear Mr. Melvin wasn't thrilled about the situation.

What the recorder did not pick up were those envelopes on the coffee table. Nita tried not to stare at them but found it impossible. Meanwhile, Earnest only sat gawking, his eyes wide and his mouth open same as they'd been at Roger Dooley's house. Nita realized how Mr. Melvin's apartment and Roger Dooley's places were alike, even in their stark contrast. Both were collectors of history, in a way, although the collections were completely different versions of a complicated past.

Nita knew it was best to just dive right in. She sat up straight and cleared her throat. "Um, Mr. Melvin, so I've been telling Earnest about your memoirs."

Mr. Melvin rolled his shoulders. He sat hat in hand, eyeing Earnest like he was a thief in a jewelry store. Earnest sat rigid beside her, staring at Nita like she'd lost her mind. Nita could only nod, hoping they could pick up where they'd left off. With the baby. Walter. She still needed to research the name. To find out if he was still alive, where he lived. What he knew about Mr. Melvin. But those envelopes had changed everything.

Mr. Melvin huffed, he was grunting more, his usual wheeze now simmering like a pot about to boil. Without a word, he got to his feet and hobbled off to the kitchen. Earnest shot her a *is-he-going-to-get-an-ax?* look with a five-alarm fire in his eyes. Nita held up her palms for him to calm down, although eyeing those letters, it was all she could do not to snatch them and run.

The floors creaked as Mr. Melvin came plodding back into the room. He had a beer in his hand and a glare leveled on Earnest. When his eyes found the coffee table, Nita held her breath.

"Either of you two ever heard of the traveling electric chair?"

Nita stifled a shiver. She glanced at Earnest, whose Adam's apple bobbed in his throat. Blocks of granite were more relaxed than her friend. She turned back to Mr. Melvin. "Um, no, can't say I have."

Mr. Melvin settled into his chair. He took his time, wiping at something in his lap, letting his odd conversation starter sit in the room. "Well," he said finally with a roll of the hand. "I shouldn't have to explain it too much. They hauled this... contraption all over Mississippi. They'd hook it up to a generator—" he smiled at Earnest as he said this—" and fry people, mostly black folks, then pack up and get on their way to the next town."

Nita scribbled in her pad, her pen trembling too much to be of any use. "But your case was here, right? Where you had your trial?" Nita found it hard to meet his eyes. This was a darker version of Mr. Melvin, and he seemed to keep getting darker with each tick of the clock.

He took a sip of beer, smacked his lips. "Well, yes, of course. But those two clowns, those *detectives*, we'll call them. All they wanted to do was talk about that traveling chair. You'd have thought the circus was in town to hear them say it, laughing and carrying on about the metal head piece, about what the voltage did to a man. Matter of fact, they spent the whole first day going on about it."

Earnest scooted forward. "They kept you the whole day?"

Nita looked at Earnest like she'd forgotten he was there. Mr. Melvin gave him a broad smile. "Son. Yes, the whole day. And they were just getting warmed up, too."

Nita rubbed her arms. She held her breath as Mr. Melvin described the effects an electric chair had on the human body. Earnest scooted forward, both entranced and terrified, as Mr. Melvin spoke in vivid detail about the jolts of current, heart stoppage, and the loss of bladder function.

"They said the traveling chair was on the way up, sure as we spoke. Said maybe there'd even be a radio broadcast, stirring up the local folks. So that if the chair didn't get me I shouldn't worry, they'd have a mob a mile long, ready and waiting to string me up on the nearest tree. Said the only thing was going to save my black tail was to come clean and admit what I'd done to Mary."

Earnest groaned. Nita could almost hear him panting over there. She sat up straight, trying to appear confident. But nothing was right. She'd sure picked a fine time to bring Earnest over to Mr. Melvin's place.

The old man was in no rush to get to those envelopes. He sipped and smacked his lips. He regarded Earnest again. "You said the whole day. Ha. You wanna know how long they kept me in that room?"

Nita knew the answer was thirty-three hours, she'd read about it. But reading about a thirty-three-hour interrogation and reliving the torture in a dark room with the man who was talking in detail about the effects of an electric chair were two entirely different things. She left it up to Earnest to guess. He shrugged.

"Thirty-three hours. Thirty-three hours without food or water or a hint of hope I'd ever see daylight again. Told me if I wanted to go around dating white women, then I was going to fry or hang. Take my pick."

Nita glanced up. "Wait. They said *dating*?"

Mr. Melvin's chair wrenched as he leaned forward. Both Nita and Earnest leaned back. The old man's eyes pulsed with lunacy, his whisper reeked of beer. "Nita. They knew about me and Mary. They knew I'd done nothing to hurt her."

Nita thought about James A. Dooley. She swallowed.

He sat back and nodded. "You think I'd be alive to tell this story if they thought I was guilty? No, had nothing at all to do with guilt or innocence, my girl. This was about revenge. This was about teaching me a lesson for what I'd done."

Earnest spoke first. "But you didn't do anything wrong."

"Sure I did." The old man grinned. "I did something that terrified them. Terrified those people from the first time they saw a black man. I did what scared them more than anything else. I fell in love with one of their own."

Nita took the pen out of her mouth and tried to get something down. The cap was chewed to bits. "And you confessed because you were heartbroken over—"

"Because I was a coward!"

Spit flew from his mouth. Nita's pen fell to the floor. Earnest shook his head. Mr. Melvin drained his beer, looked at the windows, chewing on his bottom lip.

The room seemed to echo with his anger. It sank into the walls, absorbed by the faces in the frames. While outside the world continued to move ahead. Birds sang, traffic swooshed, horns honked. Nita hit the button on the recorder.

This interview was over.

Nita found her pen and got to her feet. Earnest was at the door in a flash. The old man was worn out. The day was wearing on Nita. She needed time to think, to sort things out. And that's when Mr. Hack entered the room. *Nita, the envelopes.*

She stopped. Earnest's hand remained on the doorknob. She spoke to the back of the old man's head. "Mr. Melvin, about the letters."

"What about them?" he said, as though they were junk mail.

Nita took a breath, saw Earnest looking ready to take off running down the hall. She gave him a reassuring nod. Mr. Hack, however, wasn't going anywhere.

*Ask!*

Nita cleared her throat. "I'd like to read them."

Five seconds passed. Ten. Mr. Melvin's head turned. He stared at his window, where outside the sun was falling. Inside, the faces on the wall were graying, fading to the dusk. Earnest turned the handle and opened the door. Nita waited.

Mr. Melvin cleared his throat, his eyes still at the window. He tossed a hand over the coffee table. "Take 'em, Nita. I can't do nothing with them."

Nita scooped up the envelopes, scanned the words written by a hand that took the life of the writer. Suicide notes.

"I'll have these back to you in the morning."

Mr. Melvin never moved. But when Nita had leaned over to get the letters, before she turned for the door, she thought she saw tears glistening on the old man's face.

She nodded again. "Good night, Mr. Melvin."

# CHAPTER 20

For the second time that day, Earnest and Nita relished the fresh air. Nita offered to help with the stationary bike, but Earnest said he could manage. He was no longer bouncing around, no longer bright eyed and smiling. He simply mumbled how he needed to get back home. Nita nodded. Neither of them had much to say anyway, not after talks of electric chairs and hangings. Not after learning how justice was hidden in the kitchen cabinet of a prosecutor, one who'd drowned his guilty conscience with drink because he couldn't face what he'd done.

Nita watched Earnest scoot his bike/generator down the street. Once he was gone, she rushed inside where she fell into a chair at the kitchen table.

She had the envelopes. She had two interviews to study. Everything sat in front of her, bulging, breathing, holding the answers to the questions she was dying to ask.

Who was Mary Werrins?

With a breath, Nita found the first envelope and ran a finger across the torn edge. It felt like intruding, like prying open something meant to stay between writer and reader.

Nita opened the envelope. What she found wasn't a suicide note. At least not the first one, but instead, an apology, a confession, a declaration of love written in sweeping cursive.

*My Dearest Earl,*

*I cannot begin to explain. I cannot go back and undo what has upended my life and shattered yours. My words go ignored, my fists unfelt, my voice broken from screams gone unheard. They say I'm ill, because it helps them reason. They say I have been devastated, scarred by a tragic event and unable to see reality, when they are the ones who cannot see.*

*Yes. I have been devastated. I am scarred. My own family has caused the scars. I love you, Earl, I still dream of living a life with you and our baby. I miss you dearly, but I know I cannot visit. I know you don't want to see me. But know this, I love you always. I will continue to fight for you, for our baby, for the life we dreamed, not the nightmare we are living.*

*We will have another picnic. We will laugh and I will feel the safety of my hands in yours.*

*If not here, then someplace else.*

*Yours truly and always,*

*Mary*

Nita read each letter twice. She read the heartbreaking pleas seen only by prison guards. The pleas Mr. Melvin claimed he never read. She read them a third time. Between the memoirs, the talks, the newspaper clippings, and now the letters, Nita had the pieces to her puzzle.

She paced. She cried. She fired up the loaner computer.

Time to put the pieces together.

She didn't write about the Earl Melvin everyone knew, or thought they knew, but the Earl Melvin who'd loved what he couldn't love. What was forbidden. The world he knew but Mary did not. She wrote about what he'd risked for love. About his fears. About society's fears. And what it cost him in the end.

The windows shined black with nightfall. Mr. Hack stayed on strike. Only the shudder of the refrigerator and the rush of traffic behind her thoughts. Dinner went unnoticed. Nita wrote and wrote. She wrote about Mary's hair flying in Earl Melvin's face as the car sped down the road in a desperate search for privacy. A love affair that bloomed on a country road.

For Earl, Mary's pregnancy was a timer. An hourglass on the table. A noose being crafted and measured from a tree limb. The baby was a threat to their secret.

Mary wanted to leave but Earl Melvin had refused. He was torn between running and not running. For Earl, both acts were shameful. And then Mary's parents found out. And it was too late to do much of anything. And so he lost everything. Mary. The baby. His freedom. And all he had was time. Plenty of time to think about fear and shame and regret. Plenty of time to get angry.

Nita's fingers skipped across the keys. After a while she had to plug the laptop in because the battery ran low. She wrote about Earl Melvin's broken heart. About the traveling electric chair and the threats that came for thirty-three hours in that small room.

Mr. Melvin had told her to use her fear. And so she did. She wrote about constitutional rights. About the trial and sentencing. She wrote about appeals and supreme courts. She wrote about mobs of men ready to string up Mr. Melvin from a tree. She wrote about Roger Dooley and his father's admission. She wrote about Walter Clemmons Werrins, and wondered what he knew about his father.

She had to stop at times. When the lump in her throat made

her eyes well. When she thought about the men punching and kicking Earl Melvin. The sheriff standing idle. The arrest, the interrogation, the trial, the cold solitude of twenty years in a cell. How when Earl Melvin went to jail, Mary went with him in her mind. And how when she took her life, she took his heart and never gave it back.

Mr. Melvin didn't want to face Mary in court or stand accused of something he didn't do. But he did. He never pleaded his innocence, never uttered a word except for the occasional "No" or "Yes." His court appointed lawyer never did so much as even point out how Earl Melvin and Mary had been seen together several times. All the breaks together, or how Mary had spurned the advances of a coworker. And he was the one who notified Mary's parents of their daughter's "inappropriate relationship."

Nita blew her word count to bits. And she'd blown her deadline. But deadlines and word counts seemed trivial for a piece like this. Mr. Melvin had been caged, and even after his release he was still caged, toiling away at the factory then closing himself up in his apartment. But his story would not be caged any longer. While Nita could never free Earl Melvin from the twenty years he'd spent in prison, maybe she could free him from the judgment of their town.

Earl Melvin was tried and found guilty within days. He never spoke a word against Mary Werrins. They professed their love to each other in the courtroom, under oath, after Mary Werrins' "outburst" during sentencing.

Then Nita came to the last letter. Mary Werrins' suicide. She wrote about the letters. The pain in the words. How she said she'd gone to the judge and told him. How the judge didn't care. How she was institutionalized for two years before she took her own life.

Nita spent two days polishing her piece. She set it down, got some rest. Then she reread the story. She combed through her research, every detail. And then, her fingers hovered over the SAVE button. Because, while she had written about fear, she was now feeling it.

# CHAPTER 21

Mrs. Womack asked to see Nita after class. Nita had a good idea of what it was about.

"Nita, what's going on? Is everything okay?"

Nita nodded. Outside the door, in the hallways, she heard the hustle and bustle of her classmates. Pockets of laughter and silly voices. She longed to be carefree and so unattached. But she had heavier things on her mind.

"Oh, I brought the laptop in, sorry I've had it out so long."

Mrs. Womack shot Nita a look, one Nita wasn't sure she'd seen on her teacher's face before. "Nita, you know I'm not worried about that laptop."

Nita nodded again, she went through the motions of unzipping her book bag and finding the computer. She placed the laptop on the shelf, bundled up the charger and fiddled with the adapter to give her hands something to do. Her eyes welled.

"I can't turn it in, Mrs. Womack."

"I assume you mean your piece?"

She looked away, at the wall, at the concrete. At Mr. Melvin's face. "It's too much. I mean, what was I thinking? I could write some groundbreaking piece about an innocent man fifty years ago?"

"Well Nita…"

"Sure, I know the facts, the dates and timelines. But what about him? Now that I know about what he's been through, it's… I still can't believe this happened." Nita swallowed down the lump in her throat, wiped her eyes but her voice broke and her hands shook. "I mean they knew, Mrs. Womack. They knew he was innocent and they wanted to kill him."

Mrs. Womack came over to Nita. The bell rang for lunch and Nita got herself together as the halls went quiet. After a while Nita wiped her eyes. She took a breath, blushing some because she was bawling over a story. But it was so much more now.

Mrs. Womack had her yogurt and some crackers out on her desk, but her attention was on Nita. And when she told her teacher about the house call to Roger Dooley's house, lunch was forgotten.

"Well, uh, wow."

"Yeah."

Mrs. Womack stopped and cocked her head, a glossy grin spreading across her face. "You went to that man's house?"

Nita nodded.

She shook her head. "Well, let's run through this and see where we are. Oh, and no pressure, but your fellow council in the JJS are dying to read the story."

Nita's head popped up, her already thumping heart hit a new gear. Mrs. Womack laughed. "I thought that might get your attention. Anyway, I was hoping this piece would work as your Pentip Award entry. You know, if you *ever let me see it!*"

Nita wiped her palms on her pants. "Really? This could be my entry?"

"Yes. So first, I want you to take your laptop back off the shelf. Because you're going to need if for the next few days."

Nita took the computer back off the shelf. Mrs. Womack looked satisfied. "Now, I have edits to make and only twenty minutes for lunch. Well, fifteen now. Let's get cracking, Miss Simmons."

With the deepest of breaths, Nita found her flash drive. She clutched it in her palm. She shuffled her feet and tried to recall every word of every sentence she'd written then rewritten.

*Okay, kid, this is it. Hand it over...*

Nita handed the flash drive to her teacher. "It's the one titled, *Justice in a Bottle.*"

Mrs. Womack gave her a look, once again a look Nita was not accustomed to seeing from a teacher. "Okay."

Nita nodded. She sucked in a breath. "Okay."

# CHAPTER 22

M r. Melvin sat on the front porch picking at his guitar. A slight breeze carried the bluesy strums up over Nita's head and into the treetops.

He was putting on a show, Nita thought, her steps picking up. The way he stomped his foot and strummed along, plucking the blues. Notes for the brokenhearted.

The story. Every single time she thought about Mr. Melvin in prison her whole body tightened. She thought about Mrs. Womack reading her words, shaking her head as she tried to come up with a way to tell Nita the story wasn't fit for print. But that's not what she said. Not even close.

But now, outside with the wind on her face, whatever happened with the story was secondary, because Earl Melvin was like family now.

She took a seat. And sitting next to Mr. Melvin, watching as people stopped on the sidewalk and looked up and smiled or nodded, she knew she'd done the right thing writing his story. She felt her worries floating off with his song. She took a breath and smiled. "You know, you should set your hat out on the sidewalk, for tips."

He sat back, the evening sun shining off the guitar on his lap, the cherry-wood blushing against all the nicks and scratches. The old man ducked his head to catch Nita's eyes. "You know, I'm still waiting for that apology from your mama."

Nita closed her eyes. "Yeah, you planning on living much past a hundred?"

He seemed to like the answer, judging by the smile that upended his creased lips. He shrugged, the kind of shrug a man who'd done prison time and didn't fear much else shrugged. Nita sat back, then hunched forward.

"I turned in my piece today."

Mr. Melvin fiddled with his strings. "Guess that makes me famous, huh?"

Nita closed her eyes and smiled. "I'd like you to read it."

Mr. Melvin chuckled, then his face turned serious. "That reminds me." He set the guitar against the railing. He turned the other way, leaned back and reached into his pocket. He pulled out a worn velvety pouch with a draw string. "Here, I have something for you. For sticking it out, we'll say."

Nita's lips parted. The old man shot her a wink. His eyes took on a gleam as he pulled out a pendant and held it up to the sun. A bronzed compass rose that looked all the more delicate in his calloused hand.

"I want you to have this."

Nita shook her head. A shiver slipped down her shoulders and rested in her elbows. "Mr. Melvin. I can't accept that."

"This was my great-grandmother's necklace."

"Mr. Melvin..." Sometimes, for a girl full of words, Nita wasn't sure what to say for herself. But when he set the pendant in her hand, Nita felt the weight of the piece and the hearts it had covered. Her eyes began to water. Maybe his did too.

He leaned over, so she could hear the raspy struggle as he fought for each new breath. "This was hers when she was a little girl. Back when following the North Star was more than a little significant."

Nita knew well the story of how the slaves followed the North Star to freedom by tracing the handle down the big dipper to locate Polaris, which led them home—their new home, at least. She traced her fingers over the medallion, dull from age and worn smooth from wear, making it seem even more special. Her skin prickled with goose-bumps. Her breaths quickened, because she could *feel* the history on her fingertips.

He settled back in, as though he'd given her a stick of gum and not a piece of his family history. "You're a special girl, one worthy of wearing that."

Nita wiped her eyes, admiring the pendant, just daring Mr. Hack to say something smart at a time like this. Thankfully, he didn't, and Mr. Melvin motioned to the necklace. He asked Nita to turn around, and she did, setting her hair back as Mr. Melvin scooted forward. She smelled the tobacco on his hands as he placed the heirloom around her neck and clasped the chain. The pendant felt perfect on Nita's chest. Like it belonged there.

"Thank you," she said, leaning over to hug the old man until he grunted.

For a moment nothing was said. And Nita started to think about all the terrible things that had happened to this man. She was thinking about injustice and heartbreak when he looked at her and smiled a gentle smile. "Okay, let's get a song in."

That night, Nita checked the *Crawford Chronicle* website. Tomorrow was Thursday and paper day, but sometimes Mrs. Womack kicked things off early.

Nita was astonished at what she saw.

*Justice in a Bottle* by Nita Simmons.

Nita gasped. She froze, unable to move, or do much of anything but stare at the picture that accompanied the article. One she'd snapped of Mr. Melvin, on the porch with his guitar, legs crossed and singing out to the world.

She stared at her name under the lead article on the school's website. Same as the Stallworth piece.

*This is it, Nita. We've arrived.*

"I don't know," Nita whispered, her voice full of quivers. She rubbed the pendant on her neck. She scanned the words, her own words. They were direct and confident, everything she was not at the moment.

*Don't know what, Nita? This is what we've been looking for, this is gold. You may have just blazed a path to...*

"Stop. Please stop. Go away, I can't do this right now."

*Very well.*

Nita's mother arrived home in mid conversation on her phone. Nita stepped out of her room, computer in hand. She felt like she was floating. And she wasn't sure if it was a good thing or not.

"Mom, my story. It's posted."

Nita's mother held up a hand, still speaking into the phone. "I'll have to call you back."

Her mother pocketed her phone, looked at Nita, whose eyes were wide and voice high and small.

"Goodness gracious, girl. Are you okay?"

Nita bit her lip, she nodded, then shrugged. She was not okay, far from it, she'd spent the morning talking to herself in her room. The whole world could read the story now. *Okay* was nowhere to be found.

"Well let's see here." Nita watched her mom read the headline, study the picture. She watched the glow of the monitor fill her mother's eyes as she read. She never stood up for a snack or a drink. Never made it to her room to change. She read, her purse strap still somewhere between her shoulder and her elbow as her eyes scanned the screen. As she scrolled down to read more.

Twenty minutes passed. When her mother was done, she turned to Nita, then back to the computer. "You wrote this, Nita? I mean, this... this is all you?"

Nita nodded, biting her lip. Her mother stood, looked over at the wall as if she could see through it. She finally got her purse off her arm and she took the deepest breath Nita had ever seen a person take.

"Come on," she said, snapping Nita from her daze. "I need to go talk to our neighbor."

As they started for the door, Nita smiled. If she was writing to change opinions, she was off to a good start. At least until her mother looked at her again and said.

"You went to some man's house? Over in Brentwood?"

"Earnest went with me."

"Oh my Lord, child."

Nothing could have prepared Nita for what happened next. On Thursday, she received a few pats on the back. A couple "good works" and "nice jobs." No snickering in the hallways—always a good sign. Maybe the newspaper was back to going unnoticed again.

Then came Friday, Nita stood at her locker when Mrs. Womack came slicing through the crowd, speed walking towards her. Some form of Mrs. Womack anyway, her voice was ramped up, unlike the deep and confident baritone she used to throw over a class like a blanket when things got noisy. Not only that, her teacher's eyes were wide with what could be described as panic.

"Nita, we need to talk."

Nita looked around. Obviously, her teacher meant talk in her room, because they sort of were talking at the moment. "Okay."

Mrs. Womack nodded twenty or thirty times. Nita hurried to keep up with the click clacking of her teacher's steps, following her back to class, where Mrs. Womack shut the door as the first bell rang.

Mrs. Womack broke out into a pace, wiping her hands on her skirt and talking to the floor. "I know you have class, I'll make this quick."

Nita swallowed. This was not good. It was happening all over again. You didn't make good things "quick." Quick was for getting through with bad things: ripping off Band-Aids, writing letters of apology to the principal. Everyone knew that.

"I'll just come right out with it." Mrs. Womack stopped pacing and stared at Nita. *The Washington Post* has contacted Mr. Abrams. They would like to run your piece. Not only that, they specifically... well... Nita, they specifically asked to interview you and Mr. Melvin for an accompanying piece next week."

Nita discovered that a desk came in handy for catching a fall. She opened her mouth, closed her mouth, then tried again. "*The* Washington...?"

"Post." A small smile bloomed into a white gleam on Mrs. Womack's face. She bent down, eye level with Nita. "Yes Nita, and I have a feeling there will be more. Our little website crashed this morning due to the traffic."

The door opened. Mrs. Womack didn't seem to notice, that she was in school, in a class, was a teacher even. She stood straight and brushed off her blouse. A kid Nita recognized walked in and looked at Nita and her teacher and started to back out of the room.

Mrs. Womack recovered, calling after him. "It's okay, Nelson. Please, come in."

Nelson did as he was told. He looked at Nita, then at his teacher, eyes back and forth, as though they were plotting something heinous. Then his gaze widened as he met Nita's eyes. "Hey, you're Nita Simmons, right?"

Nita nodded. She looked to Mrs. Womack for help, who was all but gushing when she said, "Get used to it, girl."

# CHAPTER 24

Nita ran home, passing joggers and even a few people on bikes as she leaped off the bus, her back pack flapping against her back as she tore down the hill to her apartment. On a scale of boring to crazy days, this one had been off the charts. She'd spent more time with Principal Abrams and Mrs. Womack than in class. And not only that, Nita's principal was no longer looking at her like he was counting the days until she was shipped off to high school. Instead he treated her like a celebrity. A school marvel. He lauded Nita's "journalistic integrity" and explained in detail how proud he was of her, praising her talent to anyone who would listen.

It didn't take an investigative journalist to see he was full of it.

Nita's shoes slapped the sidewalk as she slowed to catch her heaving breaths. She saw her now world-famous neighbor on the porch and found it hard to believe anyone had feared him.

The other night her mother had been gracious in her apology. She'd asked Mr. Melvin to forgive her and the old gruff had nodded and said of course, no problem at all. He'd said how

Nita was a special girl and she was well in her rights to be protective. Nita had simply stood there, unable to believe what she was seeing as they talked and laughed like old friends.

But now, everything had changed. At home. At school. At life. Nita fell into a seat beside him. "Mr. Melvin," she gasped. "You'll never believe what's happened."

Mr. Melvin, who'd been strumming along on his guitar, stopped and held up a hand as though he hadn't watched Nita come sprinting down the sidewalk like her hair was on fire. "Hang on, Nita, I'm working on a song here."

"Oh, sorry," Nita said, trying to tame the stampede of emotions rushing through her head. She fiddled with the pendant around her neck. Thinking what he might wear for their interview, looking him over, Nita thought her neighbor looked a bit thinner than normal, gaunt even. She chalked it up to healthy habits or the angle of the sun.

He picked through a few notes and nodded to himself, then draped his arms over the old guitar and looked at her with a lopsided smile. "Okay, Nita. What's got you so worked up?"

"Um, so...." Nita tried to collect her thoughts but everything collided and came out at once. "The story, *your* story. Well, the school website crashed and Mrs. Womack said how *The Washington Post* would like to interview you. It seems my story —sorry, *your* story—has garnered nationwide interest."

Nita tossed her arms up the way she did when she was nervous. She forced herself to stop talking. She hopped up again and paced the porch twice before plopping down again. "This is so crazy."

Her chest heaved, Nita pictured the two of them on television. Maybe Oprah would come out of retirement just for this story. Either way, she'd need to find something decent to wear, but she knew she'd wear her hair swept to the side. She would nod thoughtfully, and grimace studiously at the right times while Mr. Melvin told his tale of injustice and heartbreak. Her mother would sit in the studio audience, beaming, alongside Mrs. Womack. She could see it all now. How the attention would shift to her, and she'd deflect the praise and accolades of such a precocious journalist. But internships would line up, and by the time the documentary premiered, she'd have her pick of schools.

Nita was helpless to stop her spiraling thoughts. And where was Mr. Hack? Nita figured he should be going crazy over this. When she turned to Mr. Melvin, he was still watching her but now his smile was gone. His eyes fell to the pendant and that's when all of Nita's selfish daydreaming vanished.

Mr. Melvin shook his head. "I'm not doing no more interviews."

"What?"

"You heard me, Nita. I've told my story. I'm done. I'm not going to keep reliving it all over again." He waved his hand at Nita. She felt like a gnat.

"But Mr. Melvin, this needs to be corrected. Did you know James Dooley thought you were innocent?"

"Little good it did me, his thoughts."

Nita's eyes went wide at her neighbor. "Isn't this what you've wanted. We've got to talk to the *Post*. We've got to get this out there."

"What I've wanted? Or you wanted?" He looked at her and shook his head. Nita wasn't about to let him get away with this. Not after he'd talked her into his apartment and into his life.

"But then why did you let me write the piece? The letters, Mr. Melvin, why are you afraid of telling your story?" The tears flooded her eyes, spilling to her cheeks. She thought about all the times she'd begged and begged her mother for a name, just a name, and before she knew it she'd blurted out the words. "You have a son out there."

He snapped his head around to face her, the yellow in his eyes a road map of vessels and clouds. He started to say something but another coughing fit came over him. He wiped at his mouth, turned away and yanked out his kerchief.

But Nita had seen it. He hadn't known.

Nita wiped her eyes. She'd let it slip. And now he coughed and coughed and knocked the guitar against the chair and it cried out with a chord. Mr. Melvin shook his head. He buried his head in his hands, muffling the pain escaping from his mouth. Nita felt less than human, how she was thinking of herself, of her opportunities when Mr. Melvin still carried so much agony in his heart.

"Mr. Melvin, I'm sorry. I didn't mean to..."

She reached for him, touched his shoulder and the old man took her hand. His rough fingers clasping over hers. He swung his sad, cloudy eyes up to Nita. "A son?"

Nita closed her eyes, nodded. "Don't you want to meet him?"

His voice was nothing but a wet hiss. "I've only dreamed about it, Nita."

Before she could stop herself, she whispered. "Me too."

# CHAPTER 25

Nita's heart thumped in her chest. She watched Mr. Melvin gaze across the street at the rows of houses, shaking his head. She gave him a moment, even as she wanted to ask about his dreams, about his son. But she could see he was struggling for breath. His eyes were more shut than open. He was drifting away, crumbling before her eyes.

Suddenly the story wasn't so important. "Mr. Melvin, I think you should see a doctor."

He blinked several times, cleared his throat and shook his head. His voice was low, strained, missing its story time fire. "No doctors. No interviews. No..." He shook his head, unable to finish the thought.

The porch planks continued to squeak with his rocking. Nita leaned forward, set her arms on her legs and sighed. "I'm sorry I told you... that."

The creaking stopped. Nita felt his eyes on the side of her face. She wasn't sure she could match his gaze. The guitar knocked against the chair as it shifted in his lap.

When he didn't say anything, Nita started to apologize

again. Not just for bringing up his son, but for everything he'd been through. Mr. Melvin rubbed his face, his wrinkles ironed out as he found his voice. "You know, I'd guess he's what, fifty-three by now."

"Wow," Nita managed. She wanted to say, *What are you waiting for?*

Mr. Melvin turned to her. She did her best to set him at ease. The moment was bigger than the cars passing along, the runners shuffling by. Again, she thought back to how she'd been afraid of him that night on the porch. Now she couldn't imagine not having him around. But she knew how hard this had to be for him, to have all this dragged out into the light again.

He set his head back. "Oh Nita. Fifty years and I wouldn't know him if I passed him on the street. He must think I'm... he must—"

"He should know the truth. About you. About his mom and what happened."

Nita felt it fighting to get out of her. To get out of him. She couldn't stand to hear him talk like that, to see him hunched over, like he'd given up on himself. At least when he was telling the story—even stories about the traveling electric chair—or playing the blues, at least then he was alive.

This should be the beginning, not the end. And with that in mind, Nita straightened up and took control. "So I'm just going to tell you. *The Post* is going to run your story. Maybe a few others. So, maybe he'll see it, or maybe they will find him. If you ever wanted to meet him, Mr. Melvin, this is your big chance."

A group of kids walked by, laughing and talking loud, their sneakers loose and smacking the sidewalk. From the porch, held by the weight of Mr. Melvin's story, Nita thought they may as well have been characters in a movie. He turned to Nita as she sat in the chair, her jaw tight and her head tilted. Finally, his shoulders slumped and he shook his head.

"You know, Mary took more out of me than any jail time could ever steal."

His words came slow, heavy with thought. Nita fought the pressing urge to whip out her recorder. She uncrossed her arms, relaxed with the fading sun. Time passed, seconds or minutes, she could no longer tell.

"She fought for you though, right? In the end?"

A few coughs before he spoke again. "They committed her after that. When she died, the paper said it was out of shame. Made it sound like I'd taken something from her and she couldn't live with it." He shook his head, trying to rid the pain from his soul. "Everything else that happened in those walls..." he shrugged, his eyes wet. "Didn't feel a thing."

A good journalist knew there were times to drop the pen and be a human being. And until that moment, with his pain soaking into her skin, Nita had never imagined a time when she could do that. She let her bag slide to the floor, stood up, launched into her old neighbor, and gave him the hardest squeeze of a hug she could muster.

He squeezed her back and Nita felt the hurt he'd kept trapped inside his body for so many years. She smelled the dust and must and spent tobacco on his shirt. She felt his bones shake and shudder. She heard him wheeze and sniffle and let out a sigh he must have been holding onto for years and years.

With his heartbeat in her ear, Nita hoped he would heal. She knew his heart would never feel the way it had around Mary Werrins, back when it must have pumped out love and life and flushed him warm when they were together, but she hoped it wasn't scarred beyond repair. She wondered how many beats had passed since he'd seen Mary. If the aching had dulled or if it reminded him with each beat, and every little sliver of time in between.

Nita's mother arrived home early, her car scraping up against the curb as Mr. Melvin was finishing up the song he'd been working on. Nita's mother sprang from her car, her sweater flapping at her waist and her purse swinging wildly with her strides.

Mr. Melvin and Nita both looked at each other.

Nita stood as her mother clambered up the stairs. She fixed her purse and fought to catch her breath. "Nita what have you gone and done, child?"

Before Nita could answer, her mother turned to Mr. Melvin and placed a hand on her heart. "Mr. Melvin, again, I had no idea. I mean, I knew it was wrong, and here I was treating you—"

Mr. Melvin held up a hand. "No need to keep apologizing, Miss Simmons. It's okay, really."

She looked from Nita to the old man, back and forth, still heaving. Finally, she settled on Nita. "I've been getting calls all day about your story."

Nita stood to let her mother slip into the seat. Nita took the railing, facing her mother and Mr. Melvin, a sight that made the day even stranger.

Her mother was all over the place. She found her phone, let her purse drop to the porch, and launched into a story. "So, first, I get a call from the *Crawford Gazette*. They tell me how you've broke this story, and I'm like, that's my girl, right? So I get on the website and find your name plastered all over the place, and I read your story *again*, and, well, I..." she stopped and wiped her forehead. Looking again at Mr. Melvin, "I'm just so ashamed for how..."

"Mom." Nita interrupted because she was so worked up. "What did the *Gazette* say?"

"Nita, I'm talking to our neighbor." She turned back to him. "Anyway, I just hope you'll find it in your heart to forgive me."

"Forgiven," Mr. Melvin snapped. Nita could tell he didn't like being fussed over so much.

"Mom," Nita said, risking the wrath, but she couldn't help herself. First *The Post*, now the *Gazette*. She couldn't help basking in the limelight of her fantasies all over again.

Her mother gave Nita a look. *The* look. The one always followed by the heavy sigh and the grimacing thing she did when speaking to bill collectors. When she spoke again her voice was stern. "Nita Simmons, I swear, you've got to be the most stubborn girl in all of Crawford. But if you must know, *The Gazette* wants to run a story on the two of you. Same as WSLS and every other TV station from here clear across to Richmond."

Nita came off the railing. She pushed her head forward. Her eyes went wide. She felt all the blood in her veins rush from her heart to her brain and flush down her limbs. She wanted to squeal and giggle and jump up and down. But then she caught sight of Mr. Melvin, an anchor in the storm, trying his best to rock to his feet. She remembered what he'd said, and she was caught between her wildest dreams and her newfound compassion.

Mr. Melvin lunged to his feet. "Well Miss Simmons, I'm certainly proud of Nita here. But I'm too old for all of this. Now, if you'll excuse me."

Nita's fingers found her pendant. Mr. Melvin picked up his guitar and shuffled for the door. She was trying to think of something to say to stop him, but with her mother, her neighbor, and the story all crashing down at once she couldn't get a word out.

And when the white WCVA news van pulled behind her mother's car, Nita needed the railing to hold herself up.

"Well, that was fast," Nita's mother said.

Mr. Melvin's guitar clunked against the post as he got moving. He yanked the door open and looked back at Nita. "I'm sorry, Nita, but I can't. You're going to have to do this without me."

Nita nodded. "Can we talk later?"

Mr. Melvin closed his eyes. "I reckon."

Then he was gone. And the press was descending. Nita recognized the well-dressed reporter as morning show favorite, Barbara Brown.

Barbara Brown stepped out in a flash of sparkles and teeth, her jaunty steps clicking and her shorn blonde hair shining in the afternoon sun.

Nita turned to her mother with a mixture of fear and fascination. Barbara Brown wore a smile as wide as the mighty James River. Her sleeveless, cream-colored dress revealed a pair of well-toned arms, the silver jewelry jangling as Barbara strode up with her microphone in hand. While no Ingrid Houston, Barbara Brown was a woman who had somewhere to be, which, Nita soon noticed as she paused at the rickety steps, somewhat unsure of her footing, was Nita's porch.

"Nita Simmons? Hi, I'm Barbara Brown, with WCVA, I spoke to your mother earlier," she paused, the smile dropping some as she looked to Nita's mother for confirmation. Nita's mother nodded. The smile returned. "I was hoping we could do an interview for our morning show tomorrow."

Nita half nodded, took a step back as Barbara Brown's driver swung out with a camera. Traffic began to slow, and Nita saw the faces in the cars craning to get a look at the old ugly brick apartment building. A few other cars pulled over to the curb, sensing something was going on. Nita was torn, too flustered by the newsman and Mr. Melvin's departure to appreciate the crystal-clear pronunciation, the commercial-quality voice addressing her.

Barbara Brown looked to the door where Mr. Melvin had gone. "Nita, as I'm sure you know, your incredible story has gone viral on Facebook and Twitter. As Virginia's first in news coverage, we at WCVA would like some insight on this fascinating piece of injustice here in Crawford. Would that be okay?"

Nita wiped her hair back, trying to make sense of what was going on. Fascinating? She was still hung up on viral. Again, Barbara Brown's piercing eyes cut to the door behind her where Mr. Melvin had disappeared. Her plastic smile never faltered as she peered over Nita's mother's shoulder. "Is Earl Melvin here? What are his thoughts about this? Is he looking to file suit against the state of Virginia?"

File suit? Nita thought she had wanted all this attention. Now it was hurling at her. Too fast, too much. Too soon and too unexpected. Another step back, into the chair. Nita took a breath, a look around. It appeared she'd written herself into a corner.

A hand found her shoulder. Nita's mother helped her to her feet and guided her to the door. There, Nita's mother stood like a shield between Nita and the world. Between Mr. Melvin's apartment and the mess Nita had brought to the porch. Nita's mother turned to Barbara Brown and her cameraman. "This has been an awfully big day for her, do you think we could talk at another time?"

Nita turned away, the image still in her head. Of Barbara Brown, on her porch, waiting for the story.

# CHAPTER 21

The phone continued to ding and buzz until Nita's mother turned it off. Nita sat at the table, the laptop open, her head in her hands, wondering what had just happened to her. Her redemption. Her fame and glory. She should have been elated. But it felt all wrong.

Nita had wanted to go next door but her mother thought Mr. Melvin needed rest. Nita knew she was right. She was worried about his coughing and ragged appearance. And she missed being next door. The warmth of his radiators. The cherry shine of his polished floors. The faces on the wall, the music. His guitar. She missed the many talks they'd shared in the privacy of his apartment.

In her room she plopped on her bed with her digital recorder. From the kitchen, she heard the familiar clank of the spoon on the pot as she listened to the recordings again and again, savoring the astonishment in her own voice and the powerful foot taps of his shoe on the floor.

At dinner, Nita's mother watched her with warm, glowing

eyes. Everyone looked at her differently now—everyone but him. Nita told her mother how she'd slipped up about Mr. Melvin's son. Her mother shrugged.

"Well, I think he should know."

"I don't know. He's, I think he's heartbroken. Still."

After dinner, Nita showed her mother the letters from Mary Werrins. She watched her mother's eyes go wide as she read them for herself. Soon Nita was feeling better. She was excited more about her mother being interested in something she was doing than with the news or the whole world reading over her words—something she still couldn't believe.

Her mother read letter after letter, holding a hand over her mouth. "Can you believe?" she said to no one at all. Nita shook her head. She still couldn't believe it. Her mother set the last letter on the table beside the bills and late notices that never seemed to end. "Do you think his son will see this, Nita? Do you think they'll meet?" Her mother's eyes went big. She grabbed Nita's wrist. "Nita, do you really think the governor will exonerate him? Because of you?"

Nita's lips parted. It wasn't something that had occurred to her. But she could get used to the pride that lit up her mother's eyes. "Oh Nita, you are something girl. Something special."

Nita was grateful for the weekend. She hoped to catch her breath without having to face the questions or pretend she was special when Mr. Melvin was the one who deserved all the attention. But Nita knew this thing would only grow. *The governor.* Just the thought of it sucked the breath right out of her.

And she was sucking wind when she heard the banging next door.

Nita peeked out the door. Down the hall, two guys snooped around Mr. Melvin's door. Nita noticed they were dressed like slobs, in sloppy polo shirts and wrinkled khakis, both with cell phones. Definitely not reporters. "Mr. Melvin. Mr. Earl Melvin."

She heard his coughing behind his door and she rushed out, down the hallway. "Could you please leave him alone?"

They spun around, leveled their interest on her. The guy with a baseball hat turned to face her. The guy with the goatee spoke first. "Hi, we're with Crime Weekly. We're following up on the story about Earl Melvin." They looked at each other.

Baseball Cap took a step towards Nita, looking to the other guy and snapping. "Hey, this is the girl. Aren't you? You're Nita Simmons."

Nita took a step back, about to turn and run when Mr. Melvin's door swung open, nearly flying off the hinges. "Out. Get out of here, now."

Nita gasped. Mr. Melvin's face was red with rage, his dull yellow eyes bulging. But it was his voice that cleared them out, deep and forceful. Enough to shake a room.

Baseball Cap backed off. "Okay, okay. Sorry, we're—" They looked past Nita, where her mother stood, her face tight and a spatula ready for action in her hand. They made a quick retreat, snapping pictures of the porch on the way out.

Nita rushed over to Mr. Melvin's side. "I'm so sorry, Mr. Melvin. I never thought it would be such a big deal."

He nodded. Then he started to speak but the words slipped from his breath. His hand slid off the doorframe and the other clutched at his chest. Nita tried to hold him up but only cushioned his fall.

Nita yelled for her mother. "Mom! Call an ambulance!"

Nita's mother was already on the phone. Nita looked back at Mr. Melvin, her vision blurring. She shook her head. "Mr. Melvin, please. Look at me. Please!"

His eyes rolled back. His face crumpled in pain as he choked for breath. Nita shook her head, furious at the men, at herself. She took her neighbor's head in her lap as he stretched out, his chest laboring for breaths he couldn't catch.

"Please, Mr. Melvin. Please."

"This is all my fault."

Nita sat with her head against her mother's arm. The doors in the waiting room opened and closed as medics and stretchers came and went. Babies cried, shoes squeaked, and voices came over the intercom, but Nita failed to register that any of this was real, how Mr. Melvin had collapsed in her arms. That he might not even be... well, she refused the thought.

Nita's mother lowered her head to find Nita's eyes. Not only did Nita feel the guilt for sending Mr. Melvin to the hospital, but it was a rare day off from work for her mother, who reached over and patted her head. "Nita, this isn't your fault. I think he's been sick for a while."

"Still," Nita said, wiping back her hair. "If I hadn't of written this piece, he wouldn't have had those jerks banging on his door. None of this would have gotten so crazy."

"He's going to be fine, Nita. He'll pull through."

Fine, Nita thought. He sure hadn't looked fine.

*Hang in there, Slugger.*

Nita sighed. "What a time for you to show up."

*Well, I've had a lot going on, looks like you've had plenty on your plate as well. Congrats, you've earned it Nita.*

"Earned what?" Nita said under her breath. "You saw what happened."

*Oh, that? Nothing you could have done. The old guy's ticker failed him.*

"No, Hack. Don't you understand? He has a broken heart."

*No. He has high blood pressure. Brought on by saturated fats and high LDL levels, probably prison food. Hey kid, we might have another...*

"Stop it. Go away."

Nita's mother squeezed her shoulder. She closed her eyes to fend off Hack, swinging her feet along the scuffed floor, thinking how she was such a weirdo and wishing she didn't talk to herself. Wishing she was more like Tamika.

Her mother scrolled though her phone. Nita eyed the clock. It was going on two hours since they'd arrived. Since the medics had carted off her neighbor, people gathered on the sidewalk, gawking as the old man was loaded into the ambulance. Now the TV's were too loud and the newspapers too wrinkled. The walls too stained and the floors too scuffed. Again, Nita felt her mother's hand on her shoulder.

Even here, in the E.R., her mother's voice had a certain pride to it. "Nita, I've always known you were a special girl, but I have to say, I thought I'd still have you to myself for a while."

"What do you mean?"

Nita's mother gave her a small smile and tapped something on her phone. Nita watched as she pulled up her own Facebook post—a link to Nita's story. She saw it had been shared over two thousand times already. Two thousand, two hundred, and forty-one to be exact.

Nita sat up. Her mother cleared her throat. "Here, read for yourself."

Nita took the phone and began reading the comments.

Wow, you must be so proud of your daughter!

That is top notch work.

She goes to my school!

Hope the governor seez this!!!

How sad this man sat in prison for twenty years. #Travesty.

Way to go, Nita!!!

Free Earl Melvin!!!

How old is she again?

Go Nita!!!

Amazing!!!

On and on it went. People were proud of her. Her mother nudged her. "That's not all. I gave the *Washington Post* permission to run the story, and the AP has picked it up as well."

Nita's mouth fell open. "What?"

"There's a real chance the governor will see this Nita. Maybe he already has."

*You're on your way, kiddo.*

Nita's skin prickled. Still hard to believe what was happening. But any excitement about the governor was short lived, tethered to the sight of Mr. Melvin lying on a stretcher. What did it matter when he was fighting for his life?

Nita rubbed her arms. "Really? What does that mean for Mr. Melvin?"

She shrugged. "It could. It might lead to exonerating him. A little late, but still."

Nita handed the phone back to her mother. She closed her eyes to soak up the tears. She couldn't do this right now. "I just want him to be okay."

"Of course. So do I, but let me just take a moment to tell you how proud I am of you." She held up the phone. "Not because you're an excellent writer, or famous even," she started with a small grin. "But because you're a wonderful person, baby."

"Mom," Nita said, her eyebrows up. "Pouring it on thick, don't you think?"

Nita's mother shook her head. "Not at all. Nobody in this town, myself included, gave that man a chance. We were all content to judge him." She looked off, towards the double doors to the hospital. "I feel so bad about letting him have it like I did."

"Well, you did kind of fly off the handle, there."

"But you," her mom continued, shaking her head in disbelief. Nita thought her mom looked years younger when she was excited, which didn't happen often. "You knew what was right and had the courage to prove it." She stared at Nita long and hard. "You are the strongest person I know, Nita Simmons."

Nita sat up and stretched her back. She fiddled with her pendant. She knew she had to set the record straight. "That's not true." She pointed to those double doors her mother had been eyeing. "He is, and he's in there, somewhere. And he'd better pull through."

An hour later, as Nita awaited a court show judge's conclusion in a riveting case between two dog groomers, a doctor emerged from the back. Nita stood, but nearly collapsed as her knees weren't in the mood for standing. Mr. Melvin had suffered a heart attack. He was alive and resting, grumpy as ever, but his numbers weren't good.

"He's been sick for a while. It looks like he's not taking any meds for his blood pressure or diabetes." Nita thought the doctor looked astonished he was alive at all. "He's going to have to make some major life changes."

An uphill battle, Nita thought. Scaling a mountain, really. "Can we see him?"

The doctor grimaced. Nita noticed how he wasn't much like the doctors on TV. He was short, a bit hunched over. And he looked like he'd been there for days. "Maybe tomorrow. He needs his rest. I just wanted to come out and let you know where we stand."

"Thanks."

"Great piece by the way," the doctor said to Nita with a small smile. He looked at Nita's mother. "One of the nurses recognized the name. We've all read the article. Amazing stuff. You must be proud."

Nita's mother gave her a *told-you-so* smile. "More than you can imagine."

The doctor nodded. No time for small talk. "All right. Well, come in tomorrow. We'll do our best, and hopefully have him in better shape."

With that, Nita and her mother started for the exit. The doors opened and Nita fell against her mother as a soft rain fell outside on the tarmac. She breathed the sharp smells of asphalt and diesel. She looked back one last time, to the fluorescent void of the waiting room.

As the rain picked up, Nita let herself go. She hugged her mother and sobbed. All the tears she'd been holding back came pouring out. Because she wasn't amazing or strong or even redeemed.

She just wanted to be sitting on the porch with her friend.

# CHAPTER 29

Nita spent Sunday at the hospital. The tests kept Mr. Melvin busy all morning, but by afternoon she was allowed a visit and made the most of it. She had a copy of *The Post* with her and read the piece to him while he slept. She gazed at his withered dark skin against the pristine white bed sheets. She touched his fingers and thought how they were so rough yet capable of making such beautiful music.

It was a dream come true, Nita thought, seeing her name in print, physically holding the words she'd written. She allowed herself a few minutes to savor the ink and smudges on her hands before she set the newspaper down and stood at his bedside.

"You're going to be okay, Mr. Melvin," she said, trying to gather some confidence in her voice. "First, we're going to get you well and get you out of here. Then we're going to find your son, and after that, it's on to the governor's mansion to get you exonerated."

Having spent so much time talking to Mr. Hack in her head, Nita was accustomed to one-way conversations. She paced the room, chatting up Mr. Melvin as the machines whirred and hummed. Nita nodded, she blinked, she squeezed her eyes shut because she promised herself she wouldn't cry. She set the paper by his bedside—she planned on buying several more copies—and leaned over to give him a small, gentle kiss on his temple.

Nita wondered what Mary Werrins would think of all this. Of Mr. Melvin. Of her piece. Of the sudden attention he'd spent a lifetime trying to avoid. Nita wondered if she'd ever understand. But one question kept bugging her.

How could Mary Werrins have let Mr. Melvin go to prison?

Still a loose end Nita couldn't tie. Even after Mrs. Womack explained, explicitly at times, how their relationship was forbidden, illegal even, and how Mary's family would have rather killed him. Mrs. Womack even mentioned how maybe Mary thought Mr. Melvin was safer in jail. Nita had scoffed at the thought. Who'd ever heard of such a thing?

But Mary had a guilty conscience, it was spelled out in those letters.

Nurses came and went as Nita, who had brought her laptop and finished her JJC application, read some, and even found herself humming to her old friend as he slept.

It was almost dinnertime when she walked out into the drizzle. The clouds were a thick, smothering gray, the kind that made you question if the sky had ever been blue at all. She was staring at the puddles gathering in the dips of the lot, at the oily rainbows and tire-smudged curbs, when an ambulance whipped around the tarmac and she realized she was in the middle of the road.

"Excuse me."

Nita was lost in her head but heard a deep voice calling out. Calling out to her. "Excuse me, Nita?"

Nita slowed and turned, somewhat embarrassed because she couldn't be sure if the voice had been real or in her head.

Not only that, this being famous thing would take some getting used to.

But no, the voice was real, familiar even, coming from a tall man with deep set eyes and light brown skin. He approached, as the double doors opened and yet another bleary couple entered the hospital.

"Nita Simmons?" He said, glancing around. He was dressed nice but not overly fashionable in khakis and a button down under his jacket. But it wasn't his clothes that caught her attention.

Even from a distance Nita knew those eyes by heart. Eyes she'd just left upstairs. The same deep, mahogany stare that at first glance chased you away, but if you braved the storm it rewarded you with a warm kindness that poured into you like sun through glass.

Nita forgot she was standing in the rain. The name stumbled from her lips. "Walter?"

He nodded. No one else was paying attention but Nita felt as though she was onstage. She looked around, saw people milling about, smoking, sniffling, consoling one another. Earlier, Nita had wondered if that's what it felt like visiting someone in prison.

"Hello." Walter walked up to her with a shy smile. He offered his hand and Nita took it. It was soft, unlike his father's gnarled, calloused fingers. "It's a pleasure to meet you."

Nita only nodded, her eyes never leaving his. To her, Walter's hand was like touching a piece of history. After the memoirs, the research, the letters—it felt like Walter belonged in a museum.

He looked off, up to the sky. "I heard he was here, but I kind of wanted to speak with you, actually. If that's all right? Is your mother around, to make sure it's okay?"

Nita's brain was flying. *He.* Walter's father. It took every fiber of every muscle to restrain herself from grabbing his arm and dragging him up to room 256.

The man named Walter chuckled. He thrust his hands in his pockets, took them out again. "I'm sorry to just show up like this. Do you think that would be okay?"

"No. I mean yes, of course." Nita fumbled about. Her throat wasn't working right; her head was kind of dizzy. She knew she wasn't making a stellar impression. She fought for composure, to be more like Ingrid Houston. It wasn't happening. Composure had found itself a one-way bus ticket out of town.

Walter looked to the sky again. "How about we go to the cafeteria. Are you hungry?"

They took a seat in the corner of the hospital cafeteria. Nita with a pita pocket sandwich and chips she knew she didn't have the stomach to eat. Eating seemed like a crazy idea at such a moment. When she was staring at history.

"Thanks for doing this," Walter started. "I, uh, your piece. It's remarkable." He started on his cheeseburger, stopped, then set it back on his tray. "I mean, really. I can't thank you enough for what you did."

Nita said it was no problem, like she did such things every day. But her voice told a different story, and so she wiped her hands on her lap and tried to get back on track. The initial shock, that her own words had created this monumental occasion—or mess? —was wearing off. Now the reporter needed to get back to work. She straightened up. "So, if you don't mind me asking, do you live in Virginia?"

He nodded, seemingly relieved to answer easy questions. "I do. I live in Richmond, actually."

Two hours away. All this time. Nita couldn't contain herself. "Mr...?"

"Werrins," he said, and it was all Nita could do not to fall back into the plush bench cushion at her back. Of course his name was Werrins. What else would it be? But hearing him say it, watching Mr. Melvin's eyes meld with what must be Mary's features was enough to set Nita off track. She sipped her tea and recovered.

"Right, Werrins," she said.

"You okay, Nita?'

"I don't know," Nita exhaled. "All of this is..."

"You're telling me." Walter shook his head. Nita thought he had a nice laugh, nicer than his father's. His cheeks were fuller and he seemed to observe things in a less cynical way. But it made sense, too. His father had twenty years of mistrust carved into his face.

Nita looked at him again. "Did you not know? About Earl Melvin? That he lived here in Crawford all this time?"

Walter bit into his burger. He chewed thoughtfully. It was all Nita could do not to reach across the table and shake him by the shoulders. *Let's get moving!*

"Yes, I knew, Nita. But you see, Earl Melvin wasn't my father—at least he wasn't my flesh and blood," he said. "Not until I read your story."

It sent bumps down her arms. And Nita sat there, arms chilled, chest flushing with warmth, her eyes welling with tears, shaking her head. She thought how if she never did anything with her words again, this was enough. Still, it was hard to believe. "So this whole time, you thought he... that he..."

She couldn't say it. Walter kept her eyes with his own, blinking, shaking his head. "Yes. No. I don't know, it's what I was told. Maybe my mother told me something different but I was too young. I don't remember. When my family told me the story, *their* story, I always felt... like somehow my skin was tainted. Because something terrible had happened to my mother."

Nita gasped. Her toes curled. She moved her tray to the left. One word left her mouth. "No."

"That's how it was. I wasn't just different, Nita. I was... lesser. And whatever was done to my mother lived inside of me, night and day, coursing through my veins. It was why my hair curled and my skin bore a darker shade. That's how it was explained to me."

"No." Nita said again, shaking her head, refusing. Refusing to believe what she already knew happened. And even if she hadn't known, it was clear. It sat across from her in those pain-filled, Mr. Melvin eyes of his.

Walter fiddled with his napkin, flattened the folds and smoothed it out on the table. Then he picked the napkin up and twisted it again. "After my mother passed, my grandparents took me in and raised me. They were strict and religious and set in their ways. My mother's name—Mary—was like a curse word in our house. When I was older, they told me the story. The version I knew but never fully believed."

Nita had both palms on the table, leaning into him, pleading. "Oh my. No. Walter please, tell me you know Mr. Melvin never did... anything like that." She sat back so she could breathe. Her feet were like jackhammers, her skin still crawling with those awful bumps. Nita blurted the words across the table. "You *have* to read the letters. You *have* to. You have to hear Mr. Melvin play guitar, hear him talk about your mother."

She was standing now, her voice cracking and her eyes shiny. Walter looked around as a few heads turned. Nita caught a hold of her emotions, but not her iron will. "You have to meet your father, Walter."

Walter remained seated. His food forgotten. His face was

blank. Nita opened her mouth again but couldn't find words to say. When he looked up, she saw the rising panic in his eyes. "I don't know."

Nita realized this was fifty years in the making, maybe not so easy as finding the elevator and pressing a button. But it didn't mean she was going to give up. She returned to her seat. Walter sat in his chair, seemingly deep in thought. She let the story sit in her head. But then she stood again.

She had an idea, because ideas and Nita were never separated for long. "Stay here, okay?"

Walter jerked his head up, his fear unmasked and exposed, spreading from his eyes. "Why?"

"Just stay. Please. I'll be back in five minutes" Nita started off. Then she looked over her shoulder. "Alone."

She ran to room 256, forcing herself to walk and not run as she approached so not to look like a thief.

*This is gold. Nita. Here's the plan. We interview the son, get it down and strike while the iron's hot. This is going to be big. We should contact* The Post *ASAP. Also, we may want to think about who should play you in the mini-series.*

Nita shook her head at Mr. Hack's lack of timing or compassion. She was too caught up in her head to realize she looked like a girl running through a tangle of imaginary spider webs. Her shoes screeched to a halt on the polished floors.

"Okay, first of all, *what?* Secondly, not now. Honestly Hack, can you not see? This is bigger than you and me. This is about father and son."

*See it? I've seen it all along. This is exactly the sort of thing that sells papers. Okay, hmm, for me I'm thinking Robert Redford, no, too old. Maybe that Clooney guy, no, wait. We need someone with the chops to capture my wit as well as my charm. How about Denzel?*

Nita stopped at Mr. Melvin's door. She looked around, took a breath, and figured if she was going to have a heart-to-heart with herself, it may as well be at Crawford Memorial Hospital.

"We need to talk, Mr. Hack."

*I'm all ears, kid.*

Nita marched past Mr. Melvin's room. She hated to keep Walter waiting on her, but if she didn't do what she had to do while she still had her nerve, it might not happen at all.

She found a seat on the bench near the nurse's station. She rubbed her arms. For the first time it dawned on her. This was the hospital where Mr. Melvin and Mary Werrins met. Maybe they'd roamed this same hallway, trading quick glances and secret smiles. Or maybe the whole thing had been demolished, like their relationship.

No time for that, though. A deep breath and she closed her eyes. "Mr. Hack. We've been through a lot together."

*You're telling me. We've put in the work and now it's time to cash in.*

"Please. Let me finish, Hack," Nita said, holding up a hand. A nurse slowed in passing but Nita buried her eyes into her lap before he could ask questions. She stifled a laugh, sitting there, groveling for words. Ear buds would've worked as a cover when talking to imaginary journalists. What a great idea. Late, but great.

Nita nodded to herself and started again. "We've had a good run. I can't say where I'd be without you in my head all these years. But I think it's time, Mr. Hack."

*Wait, kid. Are you trying to tell me what I think you're trying to tell me?'*

"Please don't make this harder than it has to be, Hack. But... yeah. I mean, I've made my mom proud. I've made my teacher and even my school proud."

*You've made... you've made me proud kiddo. More than you know.*

As difficult as this was, Nita couldn't help smiling. "Mr. Hack, are you crying?'

*Nonsense.*

"I never knew you had a sensitive side."

*I'm as objective as ever. Simple allergies.*

"Okay, well. What I mean is that, this is what I'd always dreamed about. When we were getting laughed out of school, about the Stallworth debacle?

*I'm still not convinced by the way. I mean, water lines? Lot of earth moving equipment for that kind of gig. Nope. Kind of fishy if you want my take.*

Nita would miss his fighting spirit, for sure. Nevertheless, she plodded ahead. "Even when everything was going on, you never gave up on me. So, I'll always owe you. But now, this thing with Mr. Melvin. It's not just a story to me. It's not a piece anymore. It's two lives we're talking about."

*Really Nita, you should write Hallmark movies. At least take a stab at a coffee commercial.*

Nita giggled, despite herself. The nurse turned back, a bemused look on his face. "Everything okay?'

Nita looked up and nodded. "Yes, sorry, I was thinking of an old joke."

The nurse eyed her with a smirk. "Gotcha. Well, if you need anything, we'll be over at the station just down the hall."

"Thank you."

Once the nurse hustled off, Nita gripped the bench. She had to do this, to spit it out. She closed her eyes and said the words. "It's time you set me free, Hack. Or maybe it's time I set you free."

Nita waited.

Nothing.

Was it that easy? Or that hard. Had he left without saying goodbye? Nita looked around, as though she might see a man in a fedora with a pencil stuck in the band skipping off down the hall.

Nothing but radio silence in her head.

Then, *You're more than ready, Nita.*

Nita took a breath. "Really?"

*Yeah kid. You've been ready for a while, frankly speaking.*

"Who's Frank?"

*It's a matter of spe—ah, you got me there, didn't you?*

Nita giggled, dabbed her eyes because it was her turn with allergies. She shook her head. "When it all went wrong, you kept me going."

*I'm going to let you in on a little secret, Nita. A trick of the trade. You ready for one last slice of cake? Some pearly wisdom? Some sweet savvy? Some—*

"Hack, spit it out."

*Okay, kid, but this might just blow your mind.*

"I don't have all day."

*Always have been an impatient one. Anyway, what I'm trying to get at is, well, it's you, Nita. It's been you all along.*

Nita sat there, waiting for it to sink in. "Huh?'

*Me. You. Us. We're one and the same. When they didn't believe, you believed in yourself. That's what got us through, kid.*

"Um, what?"

*It's that simple, kid. First name Self. Last name Confidence. Nice to meet you.* He chuckled. *Oh the look on your face, kid. But come on. You didn't know? You thought Mr. Hack was my name? Oh this is rich....*

"So does this mean I'll never get rid of you? Because if it does, I'll lose my mind. Seriously, I'll set it down right here and walk right out..."

*Nita. Nita. No worries, we're done here, okay? My work is complete. You've got the tools you need to succeed. I was just hanging around so you wouldn't give up. This is it for us, kiddo. I've been decommissioned.*

"I think I might be crazy."

*Not even close, kid.*

Nita stood. "So you'll always be around, huh?"

*Yes, Ma'am. You may not hear me, but I'll be here.*

"Well, thanks for everything."

*Thank you, kid. It's been a pleasure. Now go do what you need to do. Oh, and one more thing...*

"What's that?"

*You've got a math quiz on Monday. Don't forget, okay?*

"Ugh."

# CHAPTER 32

Nita got to her feet, unsure of how she felt about the whole Mr. Hack thing. On one hand she was proud of herself. She'd been doing all of this on her own all along. Then again, that meant she'd been talking to herself all along. She shook it off, there was no time for worrying. She needed to do what she came to do.

Nita ducked into room 256. Her soles slid across the floor of the dark room. Mr. Melvin lay like a lump on his bed and Nita was tempted to take his hand, sit by his side and listen to the whoosh of his machines. Later. Right now she needed to get back to Walter.

She found Mr. Melvin's keys on a side table and slipped them into her pocket. She took one last long glance at her neighbor, willing herself to remember everything. Even this.

"See you soon, Mr. Melvin." She turned for the hallway.

Back in the cafeteria, Nita was relieved to find Walter Werrins still sitting at the table. He stood as she crossed the floor and made her way around the tired nurses and solemn families.

"I thought you'd left," he said. "Then I thought," he rubbed his hands on his pants, "maybe you could be bringing him down here and I thought about leaving."

Nita closed her eyes and smiled. "He's resting. But trust me, you'll want to meet your father. When you're ready. He's really something."

Walter smiled. Nita liked his smile, it was shy and bright all at the same time. Mary Werrins must have been something, too. Then Walter's eyes fell to the keys in Nita's hands. "Okay, so what's going on?"

"Well, did you drive here?"

Walter nodded.

"Good. We're going to your father's apartment."

Nita motioned to her right and Walter pulled the car to the curb. Of course, Nita knew it wasn't wise to jump in a stranger's car, but after their talk in the cafeteria, he hardly felt like a stranger.

Once they stopped, Walter lowered his head and peeked up at the porch. He seemed content to sit in the car, eyeing the house as though the rooms contained both traps and treasures. Nita jingled Mr. Melvin's faded leather key chain with the several worn keys on the ring.

"Well, come on."

Walter Werrins shook his head. Nita sighed. "How about to the porch, at least? Seems kind of fitting in a way."

Walter Werrins regarded Nita. A slow smile crept across his lips. "He didn't stand a chance with you, did he?"

Nita smiled. "Nope. Now come on."

Walter moved like a man wading in the rapids. He climbed the steps with care, taking everything in as the planks squeaked beneath them. Nita led the way to her neighbor's rocking chair. "He liked to play guitar out here."

"So he was pretty good?"

"Oh yeah. He's like Mississippi John something or other."

Walter's brow wrinkled with his smile. "Hurt."

"Yep, that's the one." Nita nodded. Walter slowly lowered himself into the rocker, where he rubbed the worn arms of the chair, getting acquainted with its movements. Once he was settled in, Nita hurried off to grab the letters.

Mr. Melvin had more keys than a school custodian, but after several tries, Nita found the one that turned. A click and she opened the door. Nita breathed in Mr. Melvin. The familiar smells carried her back to happier times. Sure, his cooking, but also the stories and music. She glanced at the records on the shelf, to the guitar in the corner. Everything sat waiting for him to come home.

She was tempted to sit back and soak it in, but no, she was after the envelopes. She'd already taken his keys and entered his apartment, she didn't want to be a snoop. She found them where she'd returned them, on the polished wooden dinner table, along with some other, more official looking papers.

The first one had an emblem at the top. *Scott and Squires, Attorneys at Law.*

*I, Mr. Earl Melvin, of sound...*

A lump formed in her throat. It sucked the air from the room. Nita realized she was staring at a will.

Her eyes glistened as she turned away. She grabbed the envelopes and made her way to the door without seeing anything else.

Down the hall Nita began to collect herself. He was old, of course he had a will. But the thought of him in that hospital bed, the wheezing and the medication he was supposed to have been taking all along.

No, he would not die. Nita would make sure of it. She'd go next door every single day and personally shove pills into his mouth. She'd fix him healthy meals and they'd listen to records and eat apples or whatnot and discuss how the governor had his pen ready to exonerate him of everything. Mr. Melvin had a lot to do.

She wiped her face and smoothed her clothing before returning to Walter Werrins. She opened the door and breathed a sigh of relief at seeing him still there, rocking along and watching traffic. He turned to her as she opened the door.

All the hope vanished from his eyes. "Oh, is everything okay?"

Nita nodded, pulling herself together. "Yes, it's fine. It's..." she held the letters out. They shook in her grasp, and those pesky tears wouldn't stop leaking from her eyes. "Sorry."

"Here, have a seat," Walter said. While he didn't have his father's rich, low voice, his was nice all the same. Nita thought how silly she must have looked. Some big shot journalist she was, whimpering like a little girl. She might scare Walter away for good.

"Walter?" she said as he eyed the envelopes. "Do you have any children?"

He looked up. Shook his head. "No."

Nita nodded. He rocked some more and took a breath. "I guess, after everything that brought me into this world, I was too scared. I couldn't bear the thought."

"Yeah." Nita looked away to wipe her eyes again. And with the chair rocking along, it was like Mr. Melvin was still beside her. Almost.

But the rocking stopped. He turned to her again. "You know Nita, if I'd known kids could turn out like you, maybe I'd have thought differently about it."

Nita smiled. A sweet thing to say but she needed to get a

hold of herself. Time to get down to business. Because Walter Werrins was holding a pile of letters written by his mother, to his father. And she knew she had to caution him first.

"Walter, what I'm about to show you, it won't be easy to read. Trust me."

Walter Werrins took a breath big enough for the two of them. Nita pointed out the first letter. Walter picked up the letter and stared at his mother's cursive handwriting. Nita stood, and Walter never looked up.

She stepped inside to give Walter Werrins some privacy. So that he could read his mother's last words.

She shuffled through her notes. She paced. She rearranged a few sentences of her essay. She turned the television on then off several times. When she returned to the porch, Walter had the letters back in the envelopes. His eyes were red and he looked like he'd been in a boxing match. Nita wasn't doing so hot herself. Not after seeing the will on the table.

Walter got to his feet. His face was wet and blank as he looked back at the rocker then out at the street. Nita held her breath, hoping he was ready. He gripped the envelopes, wrinkling them some. It was okay, they were his now.

He looked at the door and nodded. "I think I should go in and see."

Nita managed a smile. She held the door open and led Walter down the hall to his father's apartment. His fingers skimmed the walls as his eyes roamed like he was at a museum or art gallery. Nita found the right key and opened the door.

They stood in the doorway, breathing in the oil soap and must from the old books. Walter kept shaking his head as he took the apartment in. It was a head-shaking kind of day.

Nita spoke low, as though the apartment was asleep. "He's really big into history. Civil Rights and that kind of stuff."

"Of course."

Nita caught herself before she started babbling. While she could have talked day and night about Mr. Melvin, she knew it was best to let Walter have this moment. So they stood there, the floors shining and the pictures gleaming, as Walter Werrins entered his father's apartment.

Even as Mary was long gone and Mr. Melvin was in the hospital, Nita couldn't help feeling like they were somehow together, living in the form of this man who was made to believe his life was the result of a horrible sin.

He studied the faces on the wall, kneeling and pointing when he found a picture near the corner, where the living room met the dining room. He reached down and took it off the wall for a closer look. An old group photo in front of the hospital.

"Look, that's her," he said, and Nita kneeled beside Walter. "That's my mom."

Chills flooded Nita's arms as Walter pointed to a pretty lady at the end of the first row, to the left of a young and smiling Earl Melvin. Nita blinked and focused on the black and white picture. It was a little grainy, but Nita could see why Mr. Melvin was so crazy about her. Mary's smile stood out from the black and white photograph. It was free and open and contagious through time. Nita looked to Walter and he nodded. He saw it too.

Walter set the picture back on the wall. He roamed the shelves but after a while they sat. Nita on the couch, and Walter in his father's chair. Walter pulled a leg over his knee, gestured to the guitar in the corner.

"So he's really good, huh?"

Nita nodded. Her eyes followed Walter's. "That's Wilma."

He looked at Nita closer, smiling. "How long have you

known my father?"

"Well," she started. "I've lived here since last year, but we'd never spoken until a few months ago." Nita frowned, feeling a stab of shame in her stomach. "The whole town always talked about him, and what he did, including me. But he convinced me otherwise."

Walter nodded at Nita. "I can see why he chose you."

Nita looked at her lap. To be honest, she almost missed Mr. Hack. Almost. She took a deep breath. "That makes one of us."

Walter shifted in Mr. Melvin's chair. "I get the feeling you aren't enjoying your newfound fame?"

"Well, it's nice, I guess. Especially after what's been going on at school. I thought it was what I always wanted. But now, I feel like I've gotten to know this amazing man and now…"

"He's sick."

"Yeah."

They let it hang there for a moment. Nita looked at the record player and thought about all the things her neighbor had taught her. And then, she looked at his son. A gentler version of the man himself.

"Walter?"

"Yes?"

"Um. I think Mr. Melvin was writing a will. It's over there on the table."

Walter looked towards the kitchen. Nita tried to guess what was going through his mind. How he'd finally found out the truth about his parents and now it was too late. Or was it?

"Walter?"

He closed his eyes with a slight nod. "I think I know what you're going to say."

"Maybe we should get back to the hospital."

A small, sad smile emerged on his face. "Yeah. I think you're right."

# CHAPTER 34

When they stepped out onto the porch, Earnest was cruising down the sidewalk on his bike, his usual basket of junk tied down to the back. Never big on social skills, Earnest saw Walter Werrins, skidded to a stop, and stood staring.

Nita waved him over.

"Hey," he said, using a hand to shield the sun that had slipped under the clouds.

Nita looked at Walter. "Earnest, this is Walter Werrins. Walter, this is Earnest Calloway."

Earnest hopped off his bike, walked over, and then stopped. His eyes went round as he put it together. Nita chuckled. "Yes, *that* Walter Werrins."

Walter Werrins stepped forward. "Pleased to meet you."

Nita explained what was going on and Earnest—still staring at Walter Werrins like he was a Space Lobster—nodded like crazy. He was almost as excited as she was about the whole thing.

Nita looked at Walter. "Do you mind if he comes along?"

He shrugged. "Fine with me, but are you kids allowed to ride around town with random strangers?"

"You're most definitely not random. And you're no stranger, Walter. Remember, I'm good friends with your father," Nita said before turning to Earnest. "As for you. No dumpsters."

Earnest smiled and saluted her. "Yes, sir. But what about my stuff?"

Nita eyed a lampshade, a computer keyboard missing several keys, and what was either an antenna or some sort of a weird looking ladder. "I think you'll be okay."

Walter shot her a puzzled look. Nita shook her head. "Long story."

The ride to the hospital was only a couple of miles, but was long enough for Walter and Earnest to bond over a love of science and junk. Earnest lit up when he found a remote-control airplane in the backseat, asking Walter several questions ranging from battery life to GPS roaming range. Nita smiled, thankful for Earnest's ability to lighten the mood with his dorkiness.

Nita entered Crawford Memorial for the third time in less than a day. She led Earnest and Walter to room 256 where they stopped at the bench where she'd said her goodbyes to Mr. Hack.

"Okay, um, I guess I should go in and warn him. I mean, not warn him but... you know."

"Probably a good idea." Walter nodded. Nita couldn't help but notice his shaky breaths, how he kept rubbing his palms on his hips. Meanwhile Earnest had his eyes on the nurses' station and the many gadgets to admire.

Nita called after him. "Earnest, no roaming."

"Yeah, yeah."

Earnest flashed a smile and Nita's heart did something weird. She thought about what Tamika had said about him being her boyfriend but shook it off. By then Earnest had plopped down beside Walter, another surprise, and by the time she started for room 256 the two of them were already talking science.

The television was on in Mr. Melvin's room. Nita found her neighbor sitting upright and watching some old sitcom she didn't recognize. He saw her and cracked a smile.

"Nita."

"Hey Mr. Melvin, how are you—?" Nita's voice caught as she remembered the will.

"Oh, well, I've been better," he said. "Suppose I've been worse, too."

Nita walked over and pulled out the keys and set them on the table. Mr. Melvin watched, hoisting his eyebrows. Nita tried her best to calm herself, but the old man could read her like a book. "Mr. Melvin, I sort of have someone outside I'd like you to meet."

"Sort of, huh?" he said with a wheeze. Even in his groggy state the old man was sharp. She watched him turn away, look out the window and sigh. "Nita, I'm not so sure..."

His once powerful voice was now a weak rasp. His face was gaunt and Nita was having trouble keeping herself together as she reached for his hand. She felt the scars and callouses and pain on his knuckles. She wasn't sure how hard to push him. She didn't want to cause him stress, for his heart or otherwise. "If you're not sure, then okay. But if you've ever wondered, which, of course you have, well... he's a lot like you, but I think he's a lot like her, too."

He turned to her. She gave his big hand a squeeze and steadied herself at his bed. She thought about how far she'd come. How a silly sinkhole piece used to mean so much to her. How she'd been afraid to show her face at school, and dreaded the thought of high school next year. Even the dues for the JJC convention. It all seemed so small now. But this, this warm hand, the cracked skin, and the pain in his eyes. This was real.

And Nita had told his story.

That's what was important. The story was about Mr. Melvin, not her or the paper or even *The Washington Post*. And somewhere along the way, Nita realized she was a journalist, a good journalist. But she was an even better friend.

She was still squeezing Mr. Melvin's hand when he closed his eyes and said, "Okay."

Nita's heart tried to fly out of her chest. "Okay?"

He nodded again. "Okay."

Nita hardly recognized the girl in the mirror. The one all fancied up like a princess with a French braid swept around her head. She wore only a hint of eyeliner, applied tastefully by her mother. The girl in the mirror looked ready to dazzle.

But the girl in the dress had never been so nervous.

She paced back and forth, taking in the view of the Potomac River from the sixth floor of her hotel room. *Her* hotel room. Nita Simmons. *Guest of Honor.*

She set her forehead against the sun-warmed glass, her quivering breaths steaming the window. She rubbed the compass rose pendant that never left her neck. She took several deep, fog-inducing breaths to steady her nerves.

Her mother smiled at her from the bed. She too wore a dress and Nita thought she looked beautiful. "I don't need to say it, do I Nita?"

Nita turned back to her mother and smiled. "I mean, you can. I never get tired of hearing it."

Nita's mother stood, came behind her and took her by the

shoulders. "I am so proud to be your mother Miss Nita Simmons. Guest of Honor."

Nita felt her eyes welling up and laughed. She waved her hands at her face. "Don't make me cry again, Mom."

Her mother laughed, too. She sidled up beside Nita at the window, taking her turn to admire the Potomac. Before that day, neither Nita or her mother had ever been to the nation's capital. They had spent the warm, summery morning touring the museums and seeing the sights. Even as Nita's legs were rubbery from exhaustion and nerves, she hoped this dream would never end.

Nita Simmons was an award-winning journalist. Maybe not Pulitzer winner, (not yet, anyway), but no one made fun of her in the hallways at school. Mr. Abrams spent his spare time lauding Nita's work and espousing the great success of his little middle school newspaper. Nita had done several interviews, she'd appeared on CNN, and had even been invited to the governor's mansion, where Walter Werrins was busy with lawyers working to secure his father's legacy.

Last month, Nita secured a spot with the *Posts'* intern team. She had been presented with the Coretta Scott King Young Initiative award. She figured nothing could top the internship and the award, until a couple of days later, when she received a call from a voice she knew so well. Ingrid Houston spent half an hour telling Nita how great her piece was and how much she admired Nita's work. Nita spent the entire time on her back, kicking her legs in the air.

And then a week ago, came more good news. The Junior Journalists Club had waived her dues and placed her on scholarship, like she was some sort of prize to have on the roster. Now she was speaking at the JJC Convention, tonight. And on it went. Nita was feeling special these days. She'd been vindicated and then some. Her wildest dreams had come true.

But she missed her neighbor.

His apartment was empty. A room that held little more than an echo as Walter had removed its contents, per his father's will. Nita was shocked to learn the guitar and record collection had been bequeathed to her. And his rocking chair, hers too. After a bidding war, the memoirs had gone to a publisher.

The town couldn't get enough of the story. Rumors of books and movies were rampant. His funeral had been a major event. But Nita only wanted to be in his apartment, sharing pork chops and talking music with him again.

She'd figured things out. How he'd been sick and known his life was coming to an end. Maybe he'd chosen Nita for convenience, but with the pendant between her fingers she hoped it was more than that.

Tonight, in mere minutes, Nita Simmons would take the podium and address the crowd. She would talk about her story, *Justice in a Bottle*. Mr. Melvin's story. She'd tell all the shining faces how she'd brought injustice to light, how she'd researched and fought and dragged the dark, ugly secrets of the past out to a beacon of truth.

They'd think she was something special. A prodigy. A girl wise beyond her years. And Nita couldn't say she didn't enjoy it, even if she knew the truth. She was fine with the truth. She'd been a girl who'd lost her way, one who spoke to a voice in her head. And then she'd met a friend, a gentle soul who'd helped her believe in herself and fend off the fears of failure. He'd taught her lessons she never would have learned otherwise.

"Nita, you almost ready?"

Nita glanced at her mother, who smiled so often these days. She looked so pretty in her makeup and dress, beaming with pride. Nita took one last look back to the mirror, and she recognized the confident girl staring back at her. She saw a journalist. Someone who would continue the fight, and always seek the truth. But most of all, she saw someone who would always give it her best and believe in herself.

Turning to leave, Nita heard the deep, gruff voice of her friend.

*Don't let them get to you, Nita.*

"I won't Mr. Melvin. I won't."

# ACKNOWLEDGMENTS

So many people helped this book find its way. I am grateful to each of them.

Special thanks to Diane Fanning, for still believing in me after reading and rereading so many terrible manuscripts. To Betsy Ashton, whose kind words and encouragement early on gave me the confidence to continue. My thanks and love to Nana—my favorite beta reader. To Charli Mills and the incredible support of the CarrotRanch community. To the regulars over at the Writer's Digest weekly prompt forums. To all my supportive writer friends whose kind words have pushed me keep writing.

Thanks to the Immortal-Works team. You guys changed my life. I'm forever grateful Staci Olsen liked my story (#Pitmad does work!). And a big thanks to Holli Anderson, whose skillful touch brought Justice to life.

Lastly, thank you to my wife, Anne, who sees something in me I don't see. And to my son, Simon, who's already working on his first novel.

# ABOUT THE AUTHOR

Pete Fanning can be found on his fiction blog, www.lunchbreakfiction.com, where he's posted nearly 200 flash fiction stories. He lives in Virginia with his wife, son and their two dogs.

This has been an
Immortal Production